Love Games
Trilogy

J.F. Lowe

This page is intentionally left blank

Love Games Trilogy
J.F. Lowe
Published by J.F. Lowe
Copyright © 2020 J.F. Lowe
Edited by Kallee Wright
EBook ISBN: 978-0648737-4-2
IBSN: 978-0-6487537-5-9
Cover images: Canva
Cover created by J.F. Lowe

Warning: The contents of this book for a mature audience

Dedication

To the staff Gladesville Bayview Hotel, your staff made me feel like part of the family. Lots of beers, many laughs and my home away from home when writing. I will miss you all.

To the women that inspired me to keep writing even when it seemed impossible. Shayla, Audrey, Meredith and Leslie you are absolutely amazing.

Last but not least to my to my wonderful husband Robbie, who reminded me that we all have fears and pasts but that is exactly what it is, the past. The past can only hurt you if you let yourself relive it. You taught me to live for now. I love you xo

Married

Games

This page is intentionally left blank

Prologue

As the prisms of light filter through our bedroom door, the sound of my husband's light snore beside me bears no comfort. I'm exhausted, but I don't want to close my eyes. It's not that I am afraid. Or maybe I am. But not of my husband, god no. He is the most loving, supportive and caring man I have ever met. I know he loves me and I am completely and utterly head over heels in love with Matthew. He is the kind of man that I always wished I could have my happily ever after with.

So what had happened. Why I am I laying here

wondering what had put me in the hospital? Why had four Victorian Police officers come and searched my house and threatened to take my husband away. Why did I feel like something seriously wrong had occurred. I just don't know. I know that the exhaustion is playing its part.

I watch the rise and fall of my husband's chest; maybe if I concentrate on that, I will fall into a lull and drift off to sleep. But after another hour somehow it's not as comforting as it once was. Instead, my chest feels tight, and my heart continues to race. I force myself to take a deep breath, but the anxiety rises once again. I know something is wrong. Is it me? Did I do something? Did I take something? The emergency doctor had told me my blood alcohol was 0.02 which to me was no that high. With that amount of alcohol in my system, I could still have legally driven a motor vehicle.

We had two bottles of wine between the two of us. A bottle of crisp white Sauvignon Blanc and I had barely finished my first glass of Shiraz. It had been a typical Saturday night. In fact, it was the first Saturday night in months that we had decided to stay in, have a few wines and a nice cheese platter. Cheese and wine had always been our thing. The cheese platter had had all of his favourites, a beautiful Tasmanian blue, a creamy triple Brie and apricot and almond cheese, topped off with my favourite Danish salami and line of plain and peppered crackers on each side of the board. We even had our favourite YouTube playlist running on the television in the lounge room as background noise.

So, why did I end up in hospital? Why did the police come? And why did I feel like our lives have just been turned upside down. I lay watching my husband, no it definitely isn't fear of my husband keeping me awake but maybe more fear of myself. A sinking feeling that I may have just ruined my marriage, my life and hurt the only man I have ever truly loved.

This page is intentionally left blank

Chapter 1

Sarah

Three Months Earlier…

The keys turn in the front door. He's home, my love is home. It's only been eight hours since I last saw him but each day seems to feel longer. I sit waiting to greet him as he enters our inner city five bedroom penthouse apartment. As the jingle of the keys to play, nothing sounded better than to know he was home. I was not alone anymore. Except for Baxter that is. Baxter our little fur baby, a little seven-month-old Jack Russel that from the moment we went to the breeders home he came right out and licked my foot as if a sign to say, your my human.

I am his human alright, he absolutely ignores all others when it comes to taking orders. He is a people dog but I am the only he will listen to when I tell him to sit or no or basically any other command. Then again, am the only one that he spends all his days with, as he sits by my feet while I either write or read. That where life has come to in my thirty-six year long life. I turned into everything I never thought I would be.

Gone were the days where I was a CEO of a multi-million dollar company living the high life on cruise ships travelling the world and earning a good salary as I went. My life was now isolation, novel characters and wine.

My husband finally enters our apartment,you would never think that he is a construction mogul with the way he places his filthy construction lunch box on the kitchen table. Then again, Matthew is always the hands-on kind of guy. He knows every part of his business inside and out. He still gets on the tools most days, changing out of his suit and into his high vis gear before helping out on site when needed.

Mr reliable is what I called him when we first met. Just like his routine every day when he gets home from work. He kisses me hello before heading to the veranda and disposing of this finished lemonade bottle in the bottle recycling bin. It is the same for his lunch and pretty much everything about my husband. His alarm goes off at five thirty, we both get up. He opens the wardrobe and dresses in his suit for work and I head off to make his lunch. It's the say every week, day. Two ham and cheese wraps with three snack size chocolates and a 1.25 litre bottle of sugar-free lemonade. I use to think that anybody that ate the same thing each day must be a bit strange because have the same monotonous thing would be like eating cardboard.

That was the thing though, ever since meeting my husband two years prior it was always the same. Every day during the week was the same and when he returned home at night it was more of the same. After he returns from the veranda, he kisses me lightly again before retreating to the shower. I had the same routine too. While he showered I would get up and grab a glass of wine and sit on the couch until he six o'clock when the news starts. I would rise from the couch and begin making dinner.

Day after day during the week, nothing changes and then the weekend is always just as predictable. Saturday morning breakfast out at our local cafe, caramel latte and smashed avocado on toast for me and either pancakes or corn fritters if he was feeling adventurous. After we would go and see an elderly neighbour as she had been placed in a nursing home by her children and then we would either go the local bar or head to a restaurant before heading to the bar later in the evening.

Our lives the same story week after week, like a the same song on repeat. The only change we had in our lives was a recent diagnosis of cancer for me. A lump that had appeared in my mouth a month prior to our wedding had grown and now was creating issues with my speech and not to mention ridiculously annoying as it rubs against my teeth. I had thought it was a simple mouth ulcer.

Something that would disappear after the stress of the wedding had died down. But it hadn't and eventually it got sick of it and gone to my local doctor. It took her less than five minutes before referring me off to the Ear, Nose and Throat specialist on a priority list and less than ten days before I was surgery removing the cancers.

It was another blow to my health something that I had to fight with since the early months of my life. Another cancer. Another surgery and another time in my life where the worry of making it to my next birthday begins. It was something I thought about regularly. It feels like I'm a living and breathing medical book. I had already learnt how to cope with the diagnosis after my second cancer diagnosis six years prior but this time had my husband by my side at every step. That was something I was not use to. I was used to being alone throughout the process.

The doctors, the chemotherapy, radiation and what seemed like never-ending moments of being a pin cushion. Throughout my first two cancers my former husband was never there, no family and no friends. I had been sent to the hospital seven hours away in the capital city and my former sister-in-law sat in the waiting area on the ground floor each and every time I went. But that was always the case.

I became chatty with the medical professions along the way just to keep myself from crying for each procedure. I had developed such a habit that I was on a first name basis with my local phlebotomists at the pathology lab. We made light of the fact that I was there on either a weekly or daily basis depending on the circumstances. I called her my very own vampire. She laughed everything when I said she was more real than Edward from the Twilight Saga. Then again maybe she didn't realise that at the time I just wanted to be immortal or at least be alive long enough to watch my three children grow up, get married and maybe one day make me a grandmother but I never told her that.

This time though I wasn't alone. Matthew sat beside me, holding my hand and gently rubbing my back as we waited in the admission section of the hospital. I'm not sure who was more scared and whether he was holding my hand to console me or if it made him feel better as he didn't speak. I'm not sure quite sure that he could. He had become more animated from the moment I told him that I had cancer. That day played through my head.

I sat patiently in the specialist office and told

myself that I might walk away with a few stitches today as surely he would just lance what I thought was a cyst and after the stitches dissolve and I would be back to normal.

That wasn't the case, after a careful examination and nasal camera inserted the specialist who had been all smiles at the beginning of the appointment had become sullen. He was extremely polite but I could tell that he was trying to find the words to tell me it wasn't as simple as I thought. Letting out a deep breath I'm sure he had been holding.

"Sarah, we need to take this out and immediately." He said flipping through his leather bound desk diary.

"I am going to move some things around but I will book the surgery for the morning of the eighteenth. There is no waiting for this and to be honest the severity of it won't be completely clear until I open it up and can do further exploration under general anaesthetic." He finally said as raised his head to finally look at my face.

"Umm, what am I missing here. I thought this was just an ulcer or a cyst that would be over an done with today. "

"Sarah, I believe what you have is a

mucoepidermoid carcinoma. Which is a form of cancer that affects the salivary glands. We need to do surgery and straight away."

Bile rose in my throat, cancer. No. Not again. I had already beaten cancer twice first Ewing's sarcoma in my right humerous in 2009 and then medullary carcinoma in my right breast in 2013. It can't be cancer, I can not go through that again. The doctor's voice drowned out by the sound of my heart pounding through my head.

My heart raced and my stomach continued to churn while the rest of my body seemed to be on autopilot. It must have been because I managed to leave the ear, nose and throat specialist and the 35 minutes drive through the city home before the tears finally began to fall.

"Sarah. Sarah." A shaking on my thigh brought me back to the present.

"Sarah, the nurse is here to take you up to pre-op" my husband offered his hand to help me from my seat.

"Oh, I'm sorry." I stood collecting my bag. I turned and gave my husband a kiss before following the nurse through the restricted access area.

Chapter 2

Matthew

I had known that I was all wrong for her, that I never should have touched her, but I'd been so drawn to her sweet innocence, her genuine smiles, her interest in me as a person, that I'd been unable to resist her.

She made me laugh when he'd forgotten how. She made me want to be more when I'd stopped believing in anything good. She'd pulled me out of a grim existence and had given me something to hope for. She'd made me feel when I thought my father's physical and verbal abuse had stripped me of the ability to care for anyone or anything.

She was my salvation, my reason for turning my life around when I had been so close to not giving a shit about anything and probably would have turned out just like my old man if it hadn't been for her giving me something to truly live for.

I had been stuck in a rut of work, sex and booze. My longtime friend Eden had been the only constant in my life but even then our relationship was toxic. We had met at a BDSM club in Melbourne's outer suburbs after I'd received an invitation from a childhood buddy that had gone into the Navy. He and his mates owned the club and offered me a place to relax and learn the lifestyle.

The moment I had met Eden I knew he was trouble but I couldn't help but look at him with a sense off awe. The way that women seem to flock to him. He was charismatic and from what I had learnt, a good dominant. It was only when I walked past one of the view rooms one evening that I found out he was a man that also liked to share women. I stopped by the window watching him as he in unison with another man fucked the woman fifty shades of Sunday. It was one of the most erotic things I had ever seen. It was at that moment Eden's eyes locked with mine and his silent nod became the start of a long friendship.

We shared many women of the next five years, some as one night stands and others became more long term. None of them stayed though. They always ended up telling me that they only really wanted Eden. So I was back to being alone. That was until the day I met Sarah.

She had sent through a request to the construction company I worked for at the time for a quote on bathroom renovations on her inner-city apartment. I had turned up early as usual and grabbed a coffee before heading up to her apartment. When I arrived the door had been slightly ajar. I knocked but no answer. I called out but no response. I stepped into the apartment and that's when I saw her. Headphones on in front of her laptop, in an oversized shirt white shirt, what appeared to be braless and the most granny like underwear I think I had ever seen. She was the most gorgeous woman I had ever seen.

Her foot tapping a way to whatever she was listening to which made her breast bounce. I couldn't help but stare. I watched as she picked up her glass of water absentmindedly before missing mouth completely and spilling it down her front.

She jumped from her chair. I couldn't help myself I had to laugh. She was the sexiest and clumsiest person I'd ever seen. It must be my laugh that alerted her to the fact she wasn't alone. When she turned she shrieked. My mouth went dry and I was instantly hard. It was like the wet T-shirt competition of my dreams. The beautiful full globes on full display through the wet shirt. I stepped back with my hands up to show I wasn't going to hurt her or some creepy stalker.

"I'm sorry the door was open.I'm Matthew Davidson, I have an appointment to quote on the bathroom" I stammered.

It was then she seemed to remember that she was half naked trying to cover herself with her hands. No matter how much she tried to cover the wet shirt showed everything but I wasn't exactly going to point that out because I'm sure if she looked at me properly she would have noticed the tent in my pants.

"Oh, shit. That's today," she finally said.

"Yes, eleven o'clock." I replied trying to hide my amusement at the scene in front of me.

"Umm, can you give me a minute. I'll be right back" she turned and disappeared.

That was the day I knew Sarah would one day become my wife. Two years later she did.

Now we were both successful in our own right, Sarah with her training company and then becoming a Best Seller novelist. I had landed on my feet after meeting her and seeing that anything is possible no matter what crap cards life had given you as a child. A shiver of horror ran through me at the thought of my childhood. My father had abused my mother and by the time I was eight he had decided that I was fair game too. That was until the day he finally went too far and killed my mother by throwing her into a wall one too many times and gotten a life sentence for murder.

God, I wish my mother had the strength that my wife did. My wife never gave up, she just grinned and said that only the good die young and there was no way cancer would stop her. Matthew sighed, it may not stop her but this being her third cancer certainly is taking its toll.

Initially we thought nothing of it. It was just a small lump that we thought was an ulcer that showed up about the same time as her mother did for our wedding. She laughed it off saying, "I'm glad it's only a mouth ulcer and not a stomach ulcer because spending a week with my mother is bound to give anyone an ulcer."

After that we thought nothing of it. It was only when her speech slowly started to change that she finally went to the doctors. Now I'm sitting in the family waiting room until she finishes surgery.

I got up from my seat again and started pacing. Why is this taking so long? It's been two hours already and they said she would be out by now. I check my phone. Nope nothing. No calls from recovery and no one had come out to get me yet. As I stride up to the nurse's desk the nurse holds her hand up me.

"Mr Davidson, it has only been a few minutes since you last asked, I don't have any news yet. I will let you know when I have information. Please take a seat. Or better yet the hospital cafe is just down the hall if you would like something. I will come and get you if something changes."

"Fine" I grunt before turning towards the hall.

Eden, how are you? I was wondering if you could do me a favour. I'm looking for a new car for my wife."

"Ah the illustrious Sarah, I am yet to meet. I would have meet her at your wedding if you hadn't eloped"

"Yeah, yeah you knew why, she said she would do anything to keep things from the press and her mother." I said in jest, but it was partly true the press had been following them since they had been listed as Melbourne's new power couple. Her mother was a handful but nothing compared to his family.

"So, what's on the cards my friend, something sporty fun to ride like the old days? Or are you a kept man these days and need practical?"

"Actually, I'm thinking the latest Mazda CX-8, if you have any on hand. I'd like to have it in the next week or two." Not that I was telling him but I was hoping it would become a family car for us as my work dual cab ute wasn't exactly suitable for a baby seat. I never thought I would be thinking about having a child of my own but that was Sarah. She gave me hope of having a family that I never had. I looked at my watch again and another fifteen minutes had passed. I need to find out what the hell was taking so long with Sarah's operation.

"Look mate I have to get going, flick me through an email with model details and colour." I wasn't sharing with Eden what was happening. Him further involved in our lives could only end one way. I brushed the errant thoughts of Eden aside as I stalked back to the nurse's desk.

Chapter 3

Sarah

Bloody hell that sound is annoying. I wish someone would turn off that beeping. The sound drowns out again.

BEEP… BEEP …BEEP.

I reach my hand out to swat the alarm.

"Ahh, your awake" my eyes adjust the bright lights overhead to make out the nurse beside the hospital bed.

"You're in post-op, love, the surgeon will be by shortly to tell you how it went" she said leaning over and pressing a button that finally put an end to the god awful beeping. I try to reply but my mouth doesn't seem to want to work. Noise came out but sounded nothing like words.

"Don't speak, love. Your lips and mouth are swollen. I will grab a face pack and see if we can get that inflammation down." The nurse jotted some notes in what appeared to be my chart before walking off. Bringing my hand up to my lips, I could feel what she could obviously see. Shit. I must look like a cross between Bubba from Forest Gump and a chipmunk because it all felt swollen.

"We have called your husband to let him know you are in post-op, he should be here any minute now." While she spoke the nurse attaches a jock strap device filled with ice. "Now you be sure to let me know if your in any pain as we want to nip that in the bud straight away."

I try to speak again, this time concentrating on the movement of my mouth.

"Water" barely a whisper from my lips but yet the smile from the nurse told me that she knew exactly what I wanted and she left once again returning almost immediately with a white plastic cup. As she lifted the cup to my mouth, "Sip it, slowly" the coolness of the water tingled across my lips. Just the smallest of sips was thirst quenching.

I hear him before I see him. The shuffle of feet

and the "where is she." He's angry. What happened to make him angry. I can hear it in his voice. Oh god, how long was I in surgery for? Maybe he's been in the waiting room all this time. The curtain pushes back and my specialist motions for my husband to walk past him and into the cubicle.

"Finally, anyone would think you people are trying to keep me from my wife," he huffed walk to the side of the bed and placing his hand on my shoulder.

"Mr Davidson, we are merely following hospital protocol and only allowing loved ones in once the patient is awake and stable" the doctor shook his head before lifting up the chart from the hospital bedpost.

Chapter 4

Matthew

Thankfully Sarah's surgery had gone well and I was able to take her home the next morning. The next few days I spent working from home so that I could be there for Sarah. It felt strange, I had never had to care for anyone other myself full time my entire life. But it was all worth it. Sarah is and always will be the love of my life. She may not be the first woman I ever had but she will certainly be the last.

I made soup and anything I could make that she could drink through a straw thanks to her swollen lip and made midnight trips to the twenty-four-hour takeaway store for ice cream to help reduce the swelling. Thankfully after a few days the swell had reduced and Sarah was feeling much better.

What was the best news though was the call we had been waiting for from the Ear, Nose and Throat surgeon that they had a clear margin on all fifteen tumours they removed. Also that no positive nodes were present. All which Sarah explained to me as being a fantastic result and that chemotherapy and radiation therapy would not be required.

I breathed a sigh of relief. The tension that had me wound up like a coil had finally lifted. There of course is always a chance that the cancer might return but I couldn't think of that. I had to stay positive. I had to be positive for Sarah even if the thought of it all scared the living daylights out of me.

Sarah seemed to just smile and take it in her stride but as always that was my wife. Strong.

I wanted to celebrate. Sarah just acted as if it was another day but what she hadn't known is that I had a surprise waiting for her. I'd organised it while she was in hospital and only hoped she loved the new car. Now I had to find a way to her. I wasn't the biggest romantic but for Sarah I would try anything to show her how much I love her.

"What's the plan?" She asked stepping out into the hallway.

"First, a picnic lunch." I held up a basket. She gave him a dubious look and she laughed, her eyes sparkling.

"Don't worry, I figured you might need something gentle relaxing after the past few weeks."

A grin broke across her face and I could see a bit of relief in her smile. I wondered if she thought I was going to make things out to be more than they were. The cancer scare was over and she didn't need to worry about that.

"Where are we going for our picnic?" She asked.

"To one of your favourite places," I said with a grin. I knew how much she owed this place but she a look he gave me was almost shy. We walked without talking, letting the sounds of the city be the only noise between us.

I'd always considered myself a city guy, but there were cities and then there were cities; I hadn't realised how different Melbourne was than other places until I saw it from Sarah's perspective.

When I turned, Sarah realised where we were going and smiled. Aside from the library, one of her favourite places to go was Carlton Gardens. With all of its historical buildings, sculptures and fountain made it one of the city's favourite romantic spots. Not that I'd come here much.

Sarah turned my attention back to me.

"On the really hot days, I used to take my shoes off and go wading in the water to cool off." She laughed.

I couldn't help but laugh too, as I could imagine her sitting on the edge of the fountain, book in hand and enjoying the sunshine.

I reached over and threaded my fingers through hers and we picked a spot under a couple trees and I spread a table cloth on the grass. Sarah sat down and watched as I opened the basket.

"You know I'm not great at the romantic thing, so you can't laugh at anything I brought."

She agreed, amused, but not for the reason she probably would've thought. I'd never considered how some things I took for granted, Sarah did everything when it came to meals. Sarah could see

I actually managed a decent selection, including some mild cheese, crackers and fruit. I'd also brought nice bottle of red hoping that it would help with my other surprise the car.

"When I told you this morning that I wanted to take you out, this probably wasn't what you'd had in mind, was it?" I asked as I began to pack up the leftovers.

"No, it wasn't," she answered honestly. Sarah frowned and she looked down. She put her hand on my wrist, immediately understanding how I'd taken my statement.

"It was better."

"You're really saying you aren't disappointed that I took you here with a picnic lunch instead of to some fancy restaurant?"

"Are you kidding?" She leaned closer to me, enjoying the smell of her floral perfume. "That's the sweetest thing anyone's ever done for me."

"Well then I hope that this is even better." Sheepishly I pulled the Mazda brochure from the bottom of the basket and hand it to Sarah. "You have to go and pick up the new car from the Mazda dealer, the salesman will be ready for you at any time after Tuesday."

Sarah squealed and lunched herself towards me landing kisses all over my face. I couldn't help but laugh before rolling her underneath me and taking the kiss I really wanted.

Chapter 5

Sarah

I sat at the car dealership waiting for the salesman to finish with his current customer. Eden, he seemed like a nice enough guy but he seemed to work at a snail's pace all the time. Matthew had said that all she had to do was go in and sign the papers. It was supposed to be her new car, but there was nothing about the car that I had picked. I had wanted something small and zippy and Matthew wanted practical with all the bells and whistles. So really it was a car for him. A new Mazda CX-8, with a new skyactiv-d 2.2L Diesel engine, smart city brake support and 19-inch alloy wheels. Everything he wanted, right down to the black metallic paint colour and the dark russet

Napa leather seats.

The sales man made his way towards me, his small stature giving no hint the sarcastic wit that came out of the man's mouth.

"Well hello, Sarah. A pleasure to meet you finally." I had started to wonder if his greetings had a double meaning as he had always tending to linger on the phone when he had called to set up the details about the car and the car delivery pickup at the dealership. This time he lingered when shaking my hand. It's not that he was being inappropriate but he seemed to check her out and get an all too knowing smile as he greeted me. It was like he knew me without meeting me in person ever.

"Matthew tells me you will be taking delivery of the car this morning."

"Ah yes, he said you have some paperwork for me?"

"Absolutely, come this way." The salesman motioned towards the far office which I assumed is his. As we go through the forms, the vehicle registration, insurance and sales sheet the salesman points out the various details and required signatures. Nothing that I hadn't expected except for the little touches each time that he handed his pen to sign. Feeling like touches becoming more deliberate. Just when I begin to question how much more paperwork is required Eden suddenly stands.

"Shall I take you through the features of the and a quick drive so you feel comfortable with the car before heading home?"

"Sure"

The salesman leads me towards the sign new black metallic Mazda CX-8 and opens the drivers side door before motioning me to take a seat. Leaning into the vehicle and begins to point out the various features on the steering wheel. The cruise control, Blue-tooth control functions and music settings. He stretches across in front of me brushing my breast with his arm in to point out the centre console features and then brushes past them again Retreating to stand back straight beside the open driver's door. His pants now tented with his erection and he makes no attempt to hide it. What was with this guy. Is this what he does to all women car buyers?

"You know Sarah, I have known Matthew many years now and never said anything about how beautiful you are. You really are lovely."

He knows Matthew? Since when? Why had Matthew had never mentioned him before.

"Oh, I didn't realise you knew Matthew prior to now"

"At least twenty years now. Stay where you are, I will pop in the other side and take you through the sat navigation system."

The salesman Eden rounded the car and sat in the passenger seat beside me. There is something off with this guy. I'm missing something. He gives me a feeling that I'm not sure I like. It's as if he knows something more about me then a car salesman should. As my brain trays to mull over the new information about Matthew the salesman shows me through the navigation system.

"Shall we take you for a spin before I let you go off on your own?" he says leaning over once again pressing a button place at my knee height. His hand lingers for a moment as I sit startled and wishing I hadn't worn such a short skirt. His eyes never leave me, it is as if watching to see my reactions. I place my foot on the brake and place the car into drive before easing out of the car lot.

"Where do you want me to take it?" I asked hoping that he would opt for just a quick drive around the block to prove that I could hand the car before leaving.

"Mm, there are so many places" he grinned again.

"Are you always such a cocky prick?"

His deep laugh fills the car and flush of embarrassment reddens my cheeks. "I can see why Matthew married you now. Smart, sexy and a complete brat. And as for cocky Sarah you have no idea."

I dive the car around the block and quickly returned the car lot.

"Your all good to go Sarah. Enjoy the new car. Oh, and Sarah do behave now. You wouldn't want to get in trouble with Matthew."

I turn to tell him off but he is already exiting the car. I shake my head, thank goodness that was over. It was all a bit weird, let alone creepy. His words run through my head again. Shit would I get in trouble from Matthew ? Shit, was I rude?

Chapter 6

Matthew

My phone dinged and I swiped the message open. Eden.

You have a lovely sub - E

Your talking about my wife - M

Why haven't you brought her to the club so we could share? - E

* * *

You know why, she's innocent and I'd like to keep it that way - M

The rest of the day I was restless. I'd knew I had been an idiot to let Sarah go and collect the car but the car was hers so I thought it was the right thing to do at the time. Eden. Fucking prick. He knew I would react like this. I tried to suppress the growl in my throat.

Sarah is mine. My wife. Mine.

It was as if I was trying to convince myself of things I already knew. I couldn't help it. When it came to Eden being near my wife, I felt like a child that a bully is trying to steal their toy.

"Mine" I growled.

"Sorry Sir, can I help you with something." Jeanette's voice pulling me from my jealousy.

"Shit, sorry Jeanette, I hadn't seen you standing there." God how much had she hear. Did I say it all out loud or just the last part? Fuck. I didn't want to scare her off. She had only worked for me for the past six months and actually seemed to have a brain in her head not like the one they'd sent over from the temp agency.

"It's, okay, Sir. I get possessive about things I belong to me too." Her voice reassuring that I hadn't gone too far. anything you need Sir, I'm always here for you" her heels clicking along the floor as she exited my office.

I shook my head in disgust at myself. I really need to get control of my emotions. No better yet control when it comes to Sarah. I need her to know she's mine. I will not share her.

I closed down my computer and headed home. There was only one way this was going to work and it had to start today.

*****

I watched as Sarah came through the garage door, the sway of her hips, her beautiful lush arse. The things I would love to do that arse. After the massages from my old friend I couldn't help myself. Mine.

My kiss was unapologetically rough, brutal possessive, but that was the side of me, my wife had never seen. I could see that it rocked her to the core and set her on fire. My firm lips pushed hers apart and my tongue thrust inside, delving deep and claiming her mouth in a way that declared, you are mine. She could taste his hunger, could feel his rising need, even as I maintained complete control of her like always. Cool, calm and controlled. I needed to be if I planned on keeping her from Eden.

I pressed the button for the garage door to close, and begin kissing my way down my wife's neck, I love the way she shivers under my hot breath. Her nipples visible through the thin film of her white blouse. Time to see if she how Sarah responds to the real me.

Chapter 7

Sarah

I arrived home to find Matthew already in the garage leaning against his tool bench. Had Eden already called him? And what is going on with my husband, I had never seen him so possessive. The way that he kissed me and the way we made love right there on his tool bench in the garage. It was hot. I definitely want more of where that came from. Sex with my husband was usually great and by god he has a fantastic cock. Long and thick veined shaft and bulbous head that I love to get my mouth on but there was something different about it. It was like he was trying to mark me as his.

He unzipped my skirt at the side and taking my underwear with one tug he let them float to the floor.

"Your fuck gorgeous" his words sent a rush of desire through me unlike anything I've ever felt before—until his palm slides between my legs and cups me before dragging a single thick finger through my wetness. Matthew groaned. Pure male, husky.

"You're fucking drenched for me. Jesus."

His fingertip swirls my opening, teasing me. My thighs flex, and when he dips just barely inside, my inner walls clench, greedy and wanting to be filled. What is happening to me? I push myself against his hand, and for a moment, he fills me. His hand drops away, and a cool rush of air precedes a light slap to my pussy.

"Wha—"

"My greedy wife is getting ahead of herself. I'll give you what you need, but you'll take it my way."

When I exhale sharply, another firmer smack lands in the same spot. And then he grips my hips and flips me onto my back in a single movement. My head is still spinning from the abrupt change in position, but my eyes track him as he leaves the edge of the tool bench, moves toward the tool stand box, crouches low, and then returns. He kneels at the base of the metal bench, grips my knees, and pulls me so my ass is almost hanging off the edge and my stilettos are resting on his shoulders. I'm completely and utterly exposed to him, and uncertainty fills me for a breath. He lifts something, and in the dim light of the garage, zippy ties.

I don't have time to question, because within moments he ties my ankles to the legs of the bench.

"I thought we might celebrate our new car with a bottle of wine" he says picking up a glass I hadn't noticed. It can't of been there long as glass was still frosted. Matthew lifted the glass to my lips. Mmm crisp white Sauvignon Blanc. Matthew took a sip for himself kissed me again. The mix of cool wine and his hot mouth, furthering my need.

With a grin Matthew leant back, "would you like more wine Sarah?"

"Please" not quite a beg but a plea for more. I watched Matthew take the bottle expecting him to refill the empty wine glass instead crouches down his mouth inches from my sex. His breath hot against my skin.

Suddenly, chilly liquid hits me and trickles

down . . . into his mouth. He catches the wine on his tongue, lapping up my wetness at the same time. Oh my God. Oh my God. Pleasure spikes through me as he sucks and nips and licks until I can't help but lift my hips and buck against his mouth, wanting more and more of this sensation. He stills, the pulsing in my pussy stops, and he lifts his mouth away.

"Wh—"

"You're not going to come until I give you permission. I'm going to enjoy my appetiser first."

My nipples pucker, and arousal raises goosebumps along every inch of my skin.

"Okay," I whisper.

"Please don't stop. Please." I don't know who this senseless creature is who's begging her husband to keep lavishing on her lady bits, but I honestly don't care. I expect him to resume his actions, but he does something else, something completely unexpected.

His dark eyes are locked on mine as he continues to thrust in and out with his finger and lowers his mouth to my clit. And he feasts. I'm riding high on the wave toward orgasm when a second finger pushes inside me for a moment before sliding lower. I flinch against the foreign feeling as his fingertip circles the pucker of my ass. I open my mouth to protest, but the sensation falls away and is replaced by his teeth nipping at my clit.

A moan rips from my throat as an orgasm rips through my body.

When I blink my eyes open, he's standing over me. He must have cut the ties on my legs from bench, even though I didn't realise it. His belt is undone, his pants are unzipped, and his hand is wrapped around a giant cock.

In a swift move I was impaled on his cock. A low groan came from Matthew's throat.

"Your, fucking mine," he repeated over and over again as ploughed into me. My head was spinning at the side to Matthew I had never seen before until he places his thumb between us pressing on my clit sending me over the edge once more.

Chapter 8

Matthew

As I climbed in bed that night next to Sarah, I knew she had been suspicious about the way that I had acted in the garage but I needed her. The way I needed to mark her as mine. I couldn't help myself, the thought of her near Eden had eaten at me all day. I had lost every woman I ever had feelings for to him and to have Sarah in the same proximity as him made my dominant side come out its three-year hiatus. The luckily though my actions hadn't seemed to frighten Sarah off, like I had thought it once would. Maybe the past two years together had changed things, I know it had changed me. I could no longer hold back who I really am.

It not that I wanted to dominate every aspect of her life, not that Sarah would allow that anyway but when it came to what we did in the bedroom. I needed to be in control especially when it comes to dealing with Eden.

Tomorrow, Sarah would start seeing the real me.

Chapter 9

Sarah

I woke to my husband's hand draped across my body and his rigid cock against my rear. His fingers slowly making circles around my now peaked nipples through my singlet top. There was no doubt in what my husband wanted.

"Good you're awake"

"Good morning to you too," I said wriggling my arse against him.

"Get on all fours" his instructors clear that he wanted me right then and there. So much for foreplay. Then again how long had he been playing with my nipples. Before I could manage to sit up he spoke again.

"I'm not going to ask again, Sarah."

God what's was eating him today. Surely morning sex would make a man happy. I scrambled to the side of the bed and removed my pathetic excuse for underwear. They were always the type of underwear that would put Bridget Jones to shame with. Practical that was always me. I placed my hands and knees on the bed waiting to feel my husband's fantastic cock.

He ran his hand gently over the curve of arse before skimming over my dampening pussy. "Today your going be good today, aren't you Sarah?"

Smack.Smack. Smack.

His hand came down like rapid fire over my bare arse cheeks. Never once hitting the same place.

"Answer me Sarah"

Smack. Smack. Smack again. Fuck what the hell was happening. What had he said? My arse was stingy but the heat seemed to seep into my bones and dampen my pussy further.

"Sarah, I won't ask again" his voice harsher and deeper than I had ever heard in the two years we had lived together.

I struggled to get my brain to function, it felt so

good but so wrong and what had he asked. Oh.

"Um, yes. I will be good" I finally mumbled trying to work out what was going on.

His fingers slid between my legs, with two fingers thrust into my saturated pussy.

"That's good Sarah, I like it when you do as your told. Now tell me, do like my fingers inside you. Did you like the spanking?"

It was hard to concentrate. His fingers filling me. It felt so good. I'm so close. Oh, please just a little more. Suddenly, I felt empty and the rapid-fire returned. Another five swats.

"Seems like you only respond to me when I spank you, Sarah."

Fuck.

"Yes, yes I like it."

"Good, now I want you to ask for another spanking and put Sir on the end." I was aching, aching for his finger in my pussy again or better yet his cock. God I loved his cock. Thick, long and straining towards his stomach. Just looking at it made me want to take in my mouth, licking and sucking it.

"Please can you spank me again, Sir."

I felt the smooth head of his cock run down the

crease of my arse, stopping momentarily at the place where he'd been touching just moments ago before sliding lower, where she was wet, swollen, and incredibly sensitive from my orgasm. He slid slowly inside me, but once he was buried to the hilt, he exhaled a raw groan, grabbed my waist, and began thrusting in earnest.

For long moments, I twisted in his grip, like a marionette dancing for a puppet master as he prolonged the ecstasy.

Chapter 10

Matthew

My discipline finally snapped as she wriggled her arse against my ridgid cock in bed this morning. With an unrefined curse I'd moved over her completely, pressing my chest against her back and burying my face against her neck, claiming her in a wholly primitive, ruthless way.

By god, did I love the way Sarah had responded. I felt like the supreme puppet master with the way she moved and beg to come. Her body mine.

I'd left her sleeping as I got up and showered. I

had meeting in the city at ten and needed to slip by the office for the plans before making my way over to the meeting.

I leant over and kissed her head as I left and could only hope that Sarah lost interested in my past in Eden.

Chapter 11

Sarah

I woke to find that Matthew left for work already. I knew he'd been busy on the proposal for the new high rise so I wasn't surprised to find him gone. I went about my usual morning routine. A fresh banana and coffee. The life of an author I laughed to myself as sat down at my office desk.

I was still curious to know why Eden had said he had known Matthew for almost twenty years and yet until buying this new car I had never heard of him before. I brought up safari on my MacBook. Time find out who this Eden is. As she typed in his name into the search engine an array of photos popped up.

I scrolled through the photos, jackpot. Eden Cambridge. I clicked on the photo and a news article opened.

Millionaire Car Salesman Playboy Antics

Eden Cambridge a car salesman from Melbourne's elite car yard has turn selling cars into sexcapades. With the well-known playboy caught on camera having what only could be described as kink sex in front of customers during the delivery of a car.

Onlookers were caught off guard by the midday romp as others cheered when the woman customer clearly the full service of her

delivery. Eden Cambridge or as
known in some circles as Master E,
declined to comment on his actions.
The customer who wishes not to be
named stated that "the best
customer service she had ever
received."

Well that explains the car salesman's cock
attitude towards me. I exited the article and
continued to scroll through the photos until my
breath caught. Matthew. The picture showed a
woman a provocative pose between Matthew
and Eden. I clicked on the picture to open it but
it wouldn't expand. Please enter your login.
Login for what? I exited the photo and clicked
it again. To reset password please contact
Highclere administrators.

After a few more clicks and multiple tabs
open on safari, I finally a page about Highclere.
I sat and stared at my screen. Highclere is a
BDSM club right here in Melbourne. How did I

not know this place existed?

If Matthew was photographed there does that mean? Oh my god is Matthew?

No, there was no way Matthew could have been a submissive for someone like Eden. Maybe Eden was? No, that can't be right either there was a woman in the picture, did they share?

My heart raced. Was Matthew the same man I married? Did he have a need to control, to dominate, to make me submit. Is that why he had been acting so strange the last couple of weeks?

I continued to stare at the picture of Matthew and Eden. Who is this woman? Does he still want her?

Whoever this woman was, she was the opposite of me. Her black dress clung to her slim body and her auburn hair was swept up into an elegant bun. Her makeup was smoky that made her look like a Hollywood starlet. I was nothing compared to this woman. God, look at me I thought. I could certainly use to lose a few kilos and I had Blondie hair and glasses in a really book nerd kind of way.

As I continued to stare at the photo, is that what Matthew really wanted in a wife? I had to admit, though, as my heart slowly climbed back into my chest, she was hot. Sophistication on a stick.

"It's was a long time ago" Matthew's voice came from behind me.

Shit. How much did he see. Did he hear me talking to myself too.I slapped closed my MacBook screen.

"Oh, I…" I didn't have an excuse. He saw what I was looking at. What could I say, hey my husband of the past few years I was just checking on your old hookups. Even to me I sounded crazy and jealous. But I hadn't know that I was going to find that picture. It was just there. What I really wanted to know is why Matthew never mentioned any of it before.

"Sarah, you should really leave the past in

the past. It only causes trouble by reliving old memories." He lent over and kissed me on the top of my hair.

"You were a dom?" the question popped out before I could filter.

Matthew you stepped back and lent against the door frame of my office. As he seemed to mull over his answer a slight smirk crossed lips.

"Let's just say in a former life I was," Matthew's voice seemed to deepened to a level I had never hear before.

There was so much I didn't know about him, this man who I had promised to spend the rest of my life with, to bond myself to him in a way that was irreversible.

"Why didn't you tell me before?"

"Enough Sarah, I don't want to talk about it" he didn't yell but his voice made me feel like I was a child again. I stood and lent against my desk not sure I liked feeling so small.

"Fine, I will look it up. You know I'm good

with research." I smiled to myself as I knew I would find out one way or another but I would have preferred to hear it from him. How could our marriage work if he wouldn't let me in? Be patient, I told myself.

"No, you won't" he said stepping forward lifting me to sit on the edge of the desk.

"And what's the big bad dom going to do about it?," I teased.

"Well," he said.

He moved closer to me, his hands wrapping around my waist, pushing his body into mine. "It means there will be consequences."

"Consequences to what, Matthew?"

I could feel my pussy getting wet just from the words he was saying, just from the mere suggestion that he would punish me at work.

"To disobeying me." His lips touched my skin, sliding over the hollow of my throat.

"What kind of consequences?" I moaned.

"Spankings." His hands reached down and unbuttoned my jeans, his fingers sliding against my belly. "This morning's was for pleasure, not discipline"

"Whippings." He tugged them down in the back so that my arse was exposed.

"Floggings." I moaned again as he grabbed my hips.

"Turn around, Sarah," he barked. "And bend over."

I did it immediately, bracing myself on my solid mahogany desk that was sitting on the only seconds before. He slapped me on the backside with his hand, hard and I cried out.

"You've disobeyed me," he said, and I knew he was talking about. I had googled Eden.

"And now there will be consequences."

"Yes, Matthew," I cried as another stinging slap hit my arse. He continued to spank me, harder and harder, his hand moving between my cheeks until they were red and sore and my pussy was vibrating with need.

"Stand up and turn around," he growled, and I did as I was told. He stared at me, his chest heaving. His hair was damp from the rain that had been coming down in buckets all day throughout Melbourne. Matthew grinned at me devilishly, like he was deciding just what kind of exquisite torture he was about to inflict.

"Take down your pants." I slid my jeans down to my ankles, then paused, awaiting further instructions.

"All the way." I stepped out of them.

"Now your shirt." I reached down and grabbed the bottom of my shirt and began pulling it up, the cool air conditioning hitting my torso and causing me to shiver.

Chapter 12

Matthew

I felt like a bastard. I was using sex to control my wife. Had promised my self that I wouldn't do it but when I found that she had disobey my implicit instructions about Eden. Why couldn't she leave it alone. I didn't want her looking up Eden, let alone my past.

Maybe I need to show her more of who I use to be. Made Sarah needed it.

My internal battle continue throughout dinner. I helped clean up and went and showered before settling on the couch beside her.

Turning to her I arched my eyebrow.

"Another finding love reality show, really." I honestly didn't care but it was always fun to watch her squirm when I made fun of romance shows.

"Think of it as research for me, how not to write a romance story" she laughed before leaning in.

She slid her tongue across my lower lip, one hand resting on my knee as my mouth opened. The kiss deepened for several wonderful seconds before she drew back. Her mouth was pure sin, her skin rich silk. And when I pulled her onto my lap, she curled her body around mine like we'd been made for each other.

Gripping her lush ass in my hands, I pulled her closer, felt her breasts press against my chest.

This was crazy.

Insane. I fisted my hand in her hair and tugged, drawing her back away from me. Her breath hitched. The innocence in her reaction had me hard instantly.

Fuck, I needed her.

Chapter 13

Sarah

I was tired of feeling like shit. I was tired of feeling all the bad things, honestly. The ups and downs of the past few months were taking a toll and right now, in Mathew's arms, I wanted to forget about everything except him. He made me feel wanted.

Special.

I shifted on his lap. Between my legs I could feel him grow harder and heat spread through my body, as my pussy pulsed with need. My nipples tightened when I rocked my hips and he sucked in a harsh breath.

He trailed his lips up my neck, took my diamond stud in his mouth, and bit my earlobe gently. I let a moan escape my lips and my body tensed in anticipation.

"You like this" not really a question but a statement as I shivered with delight.

His mouth claimed mine, firm and insistent, his tongue hot and demanding as he deepened the kiss. I moaned softly.

His fingers tightened at my waist and the other hand slid around to my chest. Tonight I just wanted. When he brushed over the rigid peak through of my thin cotton shirt, making me arch and moan. There was so much we had been through already, but this, the way he made me feel, was like he is I all that I need. And all that I wanted. I wanted Matthew.

"Matthew," I said on a soft groan.

"That sexy little moan you make drives me fucking crazy," he growled in my ear. Then his hands dug into my hips and holding me in place while he grinds against me.

"Are you going to tell me yet how you know Eden?'

"No" was his only reply.

"You feel so good," I murmured, resting her hands on his shoulders to brace herself over him. In this position, I was a little higher than Matthew so I could leaned down and pressed her lips to his. His tongue swept into my mouth and he wrapped his arms around me back, pulling me tight against his chest. Locked into place I couldn't move and a frustrated whimper bubbled from my throat. He swallowed it with a groan.

He devoured my mouth, sweeping his tongue inside with broad hard strokes. I tried to move my hips, to ease the ache that was pulsing between my legs but he held me firm. I growled and the damn man chuckled before pulling his head back and burying his mouth in my neck. His teeth nipped along the sensitive column, making my entire body break out in goose bumps. When I tried to move my legs, his arms locked I tighter against his body. He held my immobile, running his teeth than his tongue over my neck, up under my ear.

"Damn you," I panted. No matter how hard I tried I couldn't get any friction where I needed it. I was hot and wet and so ready for him.

"Matthew, please."

"Fuck," he growled. He dragged his lips back to my mouth and took mine in a hungry, toe curling kiss.

"Maybe we should go to our bedroom?" he managed to get out.

"Or maybe we can both stop playing games and see what happens," I told him.

His dark chuckle only fuelled the fire burning in my gut. Fine, he wanted to play dirty, I would play dirty. I leaned away from him just enough to reach the hem of my shirt and before he knew what I was doing, pulled it over my head. I hadn't put on a bra earlier.

My nipples tightened as they brushed over

his shirt covered chest and I arched back, dragging them back and forth slowly.

"Fuck," he muttered, his dark gaze lowering.

His tongue came out and he ran it over his bottom lip. Liquid heat pooled between my legs and my nipples got even harder. Every harsh breath out of his mouth made his chest rise and I moved back and forth against him. He either had to let my hips go so he could touch me or I would keep rubbing against him and drive him crazier.

A low groan ripped from my throat when I moved the hard tips over him. Maybe my plan had a flaw or two. Thankfully, Matthew loosened one arm and slid it up my side, around the front to cup my breast. When he rolled my nipple between his thumb and finger, my head fell back and I dug my nails into his shoulders. Sparks ignited and grew hotter, making a fiery trail through my veins. I had enough room to rock enough to feel him and I could feel my stomach muscles tighten.

God, I was going to get off riding him fully clothed.

"Matthew" my strangled plea fell from my lips and his jaw grew hard, but his body went harder. He loosened his other arm and slid his free hand down the front of my pants, not hesitating before he sank two fingers inside my wet core. I pushed myself up and down onto his fingers and when he crooked them just enough and pressed his thumb against my clit, raw blinding pleasure burst apart inside me so fast that I forgot how to breathe. A long low moan ripped from my throat as I clenched around his hand, my hips still rocking back and forth.

"Fucking hell, Sarah," he growled. His chest rose and fell rapidly and his fingers still moved inside me. The edge had been taken off but now I wanted him, all of him, inside me so I could do it all over again. Nothing else mattered.

"I want to ride you," I gasped, lifting myself off his lap to pull my yoga pants down. My fingers fumbled with the button on his jeans and he lifted his hips enough to let me slide them down. His cock bobbed free and I wrapped my fingers around the hard hot length. Air hissed out between his teeth when I stroked up and down slowly. His hands returned to my hips and his fingers dug into the flesh there as he guided me forward. I climbed over him, straddled his thighs and held his cock upright, enough so that I could rub the head along my slick pussy. My legs trembled and I sucked in a breath when I moved him over my clit.

"I can feel how wet you are and I know how good it's going to be when you sink down over me. Fuck Sarah, you're making me crazy." The grip on my hips tightened.

I barely held myself up, teasing his cock with my wetness, working myself up faster than I would have ever imagined. The ridges along his swollen length dragged over my clit and I rocked me hips again. Already I could feel an orgasm building.

Matthew slid his hands up and palmed my breasts, pulled both nipples between his fingers and squeezed them hard. A low groan pulled from my chest and I hovered on the edge, knowing that I was about to fall over it.

With one last drag across my clit that left me teetering on the brink, I angled my hips and sank down over his cock hard, sheathing him in one quick motion. Light exploded behind my eyes and his name ripped from my throat.

Matthew grabbed my hips and drove upward as I clenched around him. "Fuck," he ground out. "Fuck. Fuck."

His breathing grew harsher and his face was all hard lines and tense muscles. dropped my hands to his shoulders and bucked on him. Fissures of pleasure burst through my body and holy hell; I could feel it building again. I couldn't help but whimper.

Ground herself onto him and rocked my hips faster.

"Oh god, Matthew," I panted.

"Don't stop, please." He pulled me against his chest, anchoring me on top of him as he kept thrusting upward. I buried my mouth in his neck, sucked and bit and kissed. Matthew surged, growling low in his throat, and kept up the relentless rhythm. Pressure built inside me. I dragged my lips up over his hard jaw until I found his mouth.

Matthew drove his fingers into my hair, tightened them and held my head still. He kept me there, his eyes devouring me and sank into the dark depths.

Need spiralled faster and faster until I was once again poised on the brink. "Matthew." His name broke free from my lips and his eyes went almost black. "Sarah," he growled and the sound sank down into my bones. The tension inside me broke free and arched back, clenching around his cock as it throbbed, pulsed inside me.

*****

I stared at the plastic stick in my hand in shock, not sure whether I should laugh or cry at the news I'd just been delivered. Or maybe do both at the same time. That's how conflicted she felt about the entire situation. I was three weeks past due on my period. While I blamed overall stress of the cancer scare, I was never late, and it had taken me this long to gather up the courage to confirm what I already knew in her heart and face the changes already happening with her body.

I went off the pill when my first husband had gotten a vasectomy, but thought after all my body had been through that getting pregnant was something I didn't think was even feasible. Until this morning.

I swallowed hard, knowing that there wasn't really a decision to be made when I thought of it that way.

I wanted to ask Matthew more questions, to ask why he was so tight lipped about Eden. I wanted to know if only having me was enough. I wanted to reach out and take his hand, or even better: to fold myself into his arms and cling to him.

But things were too strained between Matthew and me. There was a wall between us now, dividing us. A giant elephant in the room: the fight that we'd had the other day, which apparently neither of us was ready to apologise for. And a secret as well.

I rested a hand against my stomach for a brief moment and then retracted it, hoping that he hadn't seen and that he hadn't guessed what the subconscious train of thought was that had led to that motion. I needed to tell him about the baby, but now didn't seem like the right time.

Actually, there were two secrets between us, but the other secret, I wasn't fully ready to admit even to myself. Maybe he wasn't the man I thought I'd married. Either way I had to tell him.

Chapter 14

Matthew

She finally pushed through the main door and walked inside. She stopped to glance around to find me, giving me a few precious seconds to take in how beautiful she looked in a pale blue blousy top and a pair of black capri pants.

When her gaze turned in my direction, I lifted my hand to get her attention. I watched her take a deep breath before heading my way, and as she neared, I couldn't help but think how fragile and vulnerable she looked. And very tired.

There was no easy, welcoming smile on her lips. Her eyes lacked their usual vibrancy, and her complexion looked paler than normal. There was no indication that she was happy or excited to see me. No, if anything, her expression reflected a sense of dread.

Yes, she looked as miserable as I felt, but it was the apprehension in the way she approached his table that indicated she wasn't here to confess how much she loved him and it didn't matter about my past. She slid into the chair across from me and gave me a forced smile.

"Hey."

"Hey baby," I replied, and because there was no missing the awkward tension between them, I sought to put her at ease.

"Can I get you something to eat or drink?"

"No, thanks." Her voice was too damned polite, and she looked everywhere but at me.

"This won't take long, I don't want to keep you from your work." I couldn't begin to imagine what she'd come here to tell him, but the fact that she looked so distraught and couldn't even look me in the eyes caused me great concern.

Instinct had me reaching across the table and settling my hand on top of hers. "Sarah… Talk to me please. It's killing me to have you not talk to me?" "I…" She visibly swallowed and finally meeting my gaze, unable to hide the anguish shimmering in the depths.

"I'm pregnant."

I blinked at her, shock rendering me mute. It was the last thing I'd expected to hear, and it took my brain a few extra seconds to process her words.

"You're pregnant?" I echoed dumbly as I gradually pulled my hand away from hers.

"How…" my voice trailed off, severing the stupid question of how did that happen? I knew exactly how it happened, I had fucked her every way possible since the day she'd collected the car from Eden.

I dropped my tone low to keep the conversation private, "I didn't think we, I mean you could have any more children." God the moment the words left my mouth, I felt like a prick.

"Well, apparently the doctors were wrong. I took a home pregnancy test first a few days ago, then went to my doctor yesterday to confirm the pregnancy before I said anything to you," she said, wringing her hands nervously together. "I'm about five weeks along."

I slumped back in my chair and stared at her, not knowing what to say. So many thoughts and feelings were flying through my head. Stunned disbelief. A spark of panic. And overwhelming fear, because that the reason she had brought me here to tell me she was leaving me.

I couldn't keep up with everything she was saying. I hadn't had time to digest the information as she had, and my head was spinning as I tried to come up with some kind of response.

Sarah abruptly grabbed her purse and stood up, nearly knocking down her chair in the process.

"I need to go."

"Wait." I jumped to my feet just as quickly, my heart hammering in my chest because I wasn't ready for her to go. I stepped toward her. "Sarah—"

They needed to talk... but where did I start when he still hadn't fully accepted or processed that Sarah was pregnant.

"I love you"

Her eyes wide and swimming with tears, she took a meaningful step back.

"I know," she said, her voice tight. She turned around and hurried out of the café without giving me a chance to reply.

Chapter 15

Sarah

The tears began to fall as I left the cafe. I walked aimlessly through Federation Square. I couldn't go home, not yet anyway. I'm not sure how long I had been wandering around before a voice pulled me back into reality.

"Sarah is everything okay?" Jeanette's voice full of worry.

But I could stop the tears the moment she spoke.

"Oh, sweetheart, don't cry. I'm sure whatever it is it will work out." Since when did

Jeanette care about me. She lead me to a park bench urging me to sit.

"Sarah, I know we're not close but you can talk to me. I understand what it's like to feel alone." Jeanette empathy resonated. It was exactly how I felt. Alone.

*****

It had been a few hours since I had met Matthew in the cafe and nothing had managed to change my mind that Matthew hadn't wanted the baby.

Even after talking things out with Jeanette I still wasn't convinced. She had to have faith that the world would sort things out, whatever she meant by that. She was a strange woman. When I finally arrived home Matthew had been waiting in the kitchen.

"Where have you been?" His tone abrupt.

"What the hell do you care, it's not like you want the baby"

"I never said that" his voice low.

"You didn't have to Matthew, your reaction told me everything"

"It was surprised that's all"

I stared at him. "How can you do this?" I cried.

"Do what?" he asked.

"You've taken what should have been a beautiful, happy moment for us and completely ruined it!"

He put his hands on his hips. "Just because I'm not dancing around the house, doesn't mean I'm unhappy."

"Stop lying to me." I pointed at him.

"If you don't want to have a baby with me —"

"I never said that," he roared.

"Stop telling me how I feel, Sarah."

"Well explain it, then Matthew," I replied, not willing to back down.

"I'm fucking scared, okay? I'm scared that I'm going to screw this baby up. I'm not fit to be a Dad. My own father is in prison, in case you haven't noticed."

I stood there, looking into Matthew's pained eyes and knowing immediately that he was telling her the truth.

"Oh, Matthew," she sighed. "You don't have to be scared."

"I don't exactly have a great role model to work off," Matthew said, walking to the bed and sitting on it. He put his palms flat on the bed and bowed his head.

"My childhood was… something no child should ever go through. My adult years were full of bad choices. Up until I met you, that is." He glanced at me and gave a little smile. I crossed over to the bed and sat down next to him.

"You're a good man, Matthew. A really good and kind man and I believe in you completely."

Matthew looked at me and his eyes shown with unshed tears. "I don't want to ever hurt our baby," he said softly.

"Our baby is going to have hard times and struggles just like any other person has. We can't stop that from happening. All we can do is love him. Or her." Matthew nodded again.

"I love him or her already," he whispered.

Chapter 16

Matthew

After the cluster fuck that had been the revelation that I was going to be a father I had decided it was going to be a night that I indulged my wife in every way possible. What better way than a night of romance, foot massages and sex.

I hadn't realised that changes in her body had already begun. Her breasts had become more sensitive and by god she craved sex. It had been a week since the news of the baby and I would swear the wife had turned into the most wanton creature ever. So much so that I was retrieving my kit from the club that had been in storage.

I hadn't been back to Highclere in almost two and half years but I knew that all the things I wanted for tonight would still be in the well-maintained condition thanks to a phone call earlier to my longtime friend Jackson resident dom.

As I opened the side entry door of the club a familiar voice echoed through. "She certainly is a sub, her innocence is something I haven't seen in years. Her pussy a ripe little peach just waiting to be picked. I can't wait t get my hands on Sarah again."

I shook my head. Tell me its not Eden. It would be too much of a coincidence. I know he joked with me about how much he would love to share her like we did with many other submissive over the years but fuck not Sarah. I could never share her.

I had gone to the club to get my kit bag from

the locker when I saw Eden at the bar. It was unlike him to be at the club this early unless he was training a new sub. It looked like he had been there a while, beer in hand and laughing at the conversation he was having with Jackson.

Suddenly Jackson stopped cleaning the glass in front of him and stood over bar across from Eden. "Eden, I know you have mater rights here but I'm warning you now, you mess with another masters sub there are consequences. Matthew won't take this lightly. It's not like the old days when he shared subs. He loves this one. Fuck, he married her for god's sake."

I no longer heard the reply from Eden. They didn't know I was there and I wasn't about to expose my location. I didn't need to hear anymore. I had to get out of there and now. I threw my kit back into my locker and headed for the car.

I felt hollow as drove back to my office.

How could she. My stomach churned as I replayed the conversation I overheard again and again. "Jacko mate, that was the sweetest pussy I have ever had, and fuck did she scream like a whore."

I had only been in my office a few minutes when my intercom buzzed, just as the door to my office opened.

"Your wife, Mr Davidson" my assistants voice rang through.

I couldn't deal with this now, my head was all over the place. The woman I love just crushed my heart. What's worse was I could possibly have been more forgiving it had been anyone else but Eden. Eden had shared subs with me for years before I had met Sarah but it always went the same way. The sub no longer wanted to have two doms and to be shared. Eden always got the sub. The fucker. That's why I had stepped away from the club and my so-called friend. It was only when I bought new cars or were going to the footy that I had even bother to contact him. It hadn't been the same for years. Not since I'd met Sarah.

"Matthew we need to talk about the baby" I felt as though the floor had dropped out from under me as the words left her mouth. Anger took root deep in my gut.

"There is no way that baby is mine, if you are really pregnant" I snarled.

"What are you talking about?" Sarah asked, and I almost believed that she was truly confused.

Chapter 17

Sarah

"Matthew, I never slept with Eden," I insisted. "I'm telling you, you're the only man that I slept with."

"Take your lies somewhere else," Matthew said angrily.

"I've had about enough of them! I heard him at the club. He was talking to Jackson, the bartender, telling him all about how he fucked you. How hot and tight your pussy is. I think the details were that first you rode him, and then he pounded into you and how he had you screaming like a whore? Does that sound accurate?"

I felt faint. Whore. That's what he thinks of me. I couldn't believe that Eden had said something like that. From what I knew of the man, even if we had slept together, he wasn't the type to go blabbing the details. But the truth was, we hadn't slept together, so that made it even more puzzling. I didn't know what he was trying to gain by lying about it. I swallowed hard.

"Matthew," I pleaded, taking a step closer, reaching out toward him. But Matthew stepped back, his eyes hard and his arms folded across his broad chest.

"Don't," he said warningly.

Matthew's office intercom buzzed. "Mr Davidson, the coffee you requested is here. I had them get one for your wife also, shall I bring them in, or they will go cold" Fuck, this assistant always had bad timing.

"Bring them in Jeannette" he snapped. God

this is her fault, she's just your assistant.

The door of Matthew's office opened seconds later and the click of Jeannette's heels across the floor broke the silence between Matthew and I, as Jeannette placed the coffees on his desk.

"Is there anything else I can do for you Mr Davidson?" her voice sweet and high like nails on a chalkboard.

"No thank you Jeanette, that will be all for the day. Take the rest of the day off."

"Oh, thank you Sir. Let me know if you need me at all later. I am always available for you, Sir." Janette turned leaving as quickly as she came.

I picked up my the coffee and nursed it like it was a shield to protect me from Matthew's anger. Not that it could realistically protect me from anything but I would do anything at that stage to create some distance.

He huffed out another breath. "I don't know what you think you're gaining by lying to me, but I'm not falling for it. He had all the details, Sarah, right down to that scar on your inner thigh. How else would he have known about that, if he didn't see you naked?"

"I, have no idea how he knows," I said, shaking my head. "Matthew, I swear to you, I didn't sleep with him. Please."

"What am I suppose to believe Sarah, you tell me you're pregnant and then I hear Eden spooking about how hard he fucked you." Matthew's body shook with anger as he repeatedly ran his hands through his tousled hair.

"I have never been unfaithful to you, I love you, I couldn't " my voice wavering.

"Fuck Sarah, we haven't used protection in years and now suddenly you are pregnant and I overhear that shit," he growled through his teeth before returning to his seat.

"Matthew, I"

"Just leave Sarah"

I felt like I might burst into tears at any

second. I had finally gotten up the courage to tell Matthew about the pregnancy, and now, I was regretting having done so. From the sound of things, he wanted no part in this baby's life. It was enough to have me considering giving the baby up for adoption. I wasn't sure that I could be the mother that I needed to be, knowing that the baby had been born out of such an unhappy relationship. But I knew I couldn't do that.

Chapter 18

Matthew

God I felt like a prick. I lied to her about the scar. Nothing was said about her scar but I couldn't help it. I was so angry. So hurt. I watched her leave with tears welling in her eyes, knowing I lied to her. I knew I couldn't go home to our bed tonight, I'd stay in the guest room. I couldn't face Sarah yet. I needed to apologise. God, I need to beg.

I woke the next morning and my hadn't slept hadn't be worth shit. At somewhere between misery and dawn, I decided to go for a run, hoping to clear my head. To get rid of the memory of the hurt I'd seen on her face.

The misery in her eyes gnawed me the entire five kilometres, which completely nullified any good the physical activity might have done. I deserved it though. Deserved every painful step, every sickening punch to the gut that the memories brought.

What kind of husband would say something like that to a wife he cared about? A total bastard, that was who.

Part of me thought that maybe I'd been driven by fear. Eden had gotten under my skin, made me nervous, so much that my mouth had run away with itself.

I didn't know how to handle anything about Sarah and the baby. Even the gut-wrenching need between us that should have been easy, wasn't. There was nothing more fundamental than sex, but what we had wasn't sex .

It was…everything. Sarah was my everything.

I'd gone and screwed it all up–again.

I came back from my run even more exhausted than I should have been, completely drained to the bone, an emotional wreck. After a quick shower, I collapsed face-down on my bed and sent Jeanette my secretary a text, telling her I'd be in late.

Being the professional as she was, she didn't ask questions. I had no idea what my schedule was like this morning–she hadn't updated me with meeting notes or anything important, so I had to assume there was nothing major, but things would be shuffled around regardless.

I needed sleep. I also needed to quit thinking about Eden. I no longer cared if I'm not the father of Sarah's baby. I love her too much to lose her.

Chapter 19

Sarah

Something wasn't right. I ran to the toilet once again before lifting the lid and vomiting. I never got morning sickness. I had already had three children in her previous marriage and not one day of morning sickness. That had been a long time ago now but surely my body hadn't changed that much. Another cramping feeling to the stomach and I vomited again.

"Sarah" I heard Matthew call but I couldn't answer. I couldn't move from the cold bathroom tiles that lay cold beneath me.

"Sarah, I know your home. Your keys are on the… Oh fuck" Matthew's feet came into view.

"Sarah, fuck." Matthew pushed my hair aside and lowered his head to what I can only assume was listening for my breathing.

"Sarah, talk to me, what happened" his voice full urgency.

I tried to speak but nothing came out. My whole body felt like I was asleep.

"Hello, emergency. My wife has collapsed in the bathroom." The panic in Matthews' voice clear.

My baby, please not my baby. The baby has to be ok. Please god, don't take my baby.

*****

Dark, light, dark, light. I could feel the rush of air as they pushed me through the emergency room doors.

"Thirty-six year old female, collapsed on the floor of her home. Her husband tells us she's five weeks pregnant."

"She's haemorrhaging." Darkness consumed me again.

*****

My eyes were starting to adjust to the light, and Matthew was coming into focus, his face sharpening, the look in his eyes intensifying and becoming more clear, like puzzle pieces shifting into place.

"Matthew ," I whispered, because I wanted to tell him how I felt, wanted to tell him I was sorry, sorry I had lost our baby.

"Shhh. It's okay, baby," he murmured. "Shh. It's okay."

I nodded, the tears welling in my eyes. His index finger grazed my lips, and he rested his palm on my cheek, brushing his thumb under my eye, wiping my tears.

The curtain of the emergency room cubical opened.

"Ah, your awake, I will just go and get the doctor." The nurse scurried off returning a few minutes later with an older man in green scrubs that looked like he had a long shift.

"Mrs Davidson, as you are aware you miscarried tonight and to be honest I am a little confused as your blood results came back. I'm afraid we have found something rather disturbing. Have you ever heard of the drug Mifepristone" the doctor flipped through my chart.

"No, should I have?"

"It's an abortion drug. It is taken by mouth and ends a pregnancy by blocking the action of the hormone (progesterone) that supports the pregnancy. Would there be a reason why you would take that drug, without seeking medical help?"

I inhaled, a sharp intake of breath that I held in my lungs, not trusting myself to speak without screaming. The air burned my chest as I held it as long as I could, until my head started to feel slightly woozy and I was forced to blow it slowly out of my nose. Matthew didn't say anything. I turned and looked away, biting back my tears.

"I would never harm my baby" I said through gritted teeth.

Fury rose in my chest and my free hand curled into a fist by my side, the sharp bite of my fingernails digging into my palms. How could they think I would do this.

"Mr Davidson, is there any reason you would want to harm yourself? This the third trip to the hospital you've made in only a matter of months. If you hadn't wanted to have this baby there are more appropriate ways it can be dealt with," the doctor peered over the chart with at me. How dare he. I would never.

Chapter 20

Matthew

"No that can't be right my wife wanted this baby, we both did." Matthew refuted. It can't be true, Sarah would never do that. Sarah could never take a life it just wasn't in her to do that.

"Mr Davidson, can you please take a seat outside while I speak with your wife," the doctor turned to me before pointing towards the waiting room.

" I will not be going anywhere, anything you have to say to my wife, I will be here for."

It was then that two Victorian police officers entered the emergency ward cubicle. What the hell is going on.

"Mr Davidson, if you please." The officer pointed in the direction of the waiting room.

The officer lead into the emergency room hallway. "Mr Davidson, we would like to ask you some questions about your wife. Would she have any reason to harm herself or your unborn child?"

My anger grew this bastard didn't give a shit. My wife just lost our baby. God, was it mine? Or was it Eden's. Fuck, I couldn't tell the police that. It didn't matter right now. All that mattered is that Sarah would be ok.

"Look officer, when I left for work this morning my wife had said she was feeling off like she was getting a bug of some sort, you know the usual. Nausea, diarrhoea, dizziness, headache and fever."

I knew I was lying but I can't imagine Sarah wanting to harm herself let alone her unborn baby.

The officer shook his head. "Mr Davidson, I understand that this may be difficult time for you but this sort of thing doesn't happen every day. Somethings not right with this."

"You're fucking right there. How dare you accuse my wife of doing this to herself. If you have nothing more I would like to get back to her and take her out of this hellhole." It was then I noticed that everyone had stopped to stare at us. I knew I shouldn't have sworn at the officer but I too angry not to react.

"That is all for now Mr Davidson, I will excuse your behaviour for now due to the circumstances but do not ever speak like that to me again. You are free to go."

*****

I kept glancing over at Sarah on the ride home, but she didn't dissolve into tears again. Instead, she stared numbly out the window, her eyes barely registering anything. I knew she was exhausted after that bout of crying, but I couldn't help feeling worried about her, wishing that she would show a little more life.

She was nothing more than a shell. I helped her up the elevator to our penthouse apartment and through to our bedroom. She hadn't spoke a word the whole way up.

I sighed, pulling the back the bed covers so that she could slid beneath.I didn't know what to say. I walked down the hall to the kitchen, returning with a glass of water placing on the bedside. Sarah had already turned away and drifted off to sleep.

Outside in the hallway, I leaned against the wall, closing my eyes and counting to ten. I hated to see her like this, in so much pain. I only wished that this hadn't happened to her. But I couldn't think about all of the 'what ifs' and 'could haves' now.

I watched through the open bedroom door, her light hair was a tangle on the pillow. Her lips parted as she slept. I couldn't resist anymore. I needed to feel her close to me. Stripping down as I walked into our bedroom, I climbed carefully into the bed and pulled her into my arms. Every tear felt like a knife to my heart as I pondered everything that had happened, wondering if this was all my fault.

I sighed, and for a moment, I tightened my arms around Sarah, who shifted in her sleep as though she could sense my distress. I quickly relaxed my arms, holding my breath and hoping that she kept sleeping. Fortunately, she did.

Chapter 21

Sarah

It had been three weeks since my miscarriage and nothing had been the same. Matthew had worked late almost every day and even when he did arrive home, conversations were limited to basic pleasantries. To make matters worse he'd slept in the spare room every night. It was clear he didn't believe that the lost baby hadn't been his or maybe he thought I was callous enough to kill my unborn child. Either way he hadn't wanted to be with me.

Was this the beginning of the end for our marriage?

I called Matthew and hung up as fear that our marriage might be finished too over. The moment I placed my phone back on the desk it started to ring.

I didn't allow myself time to actually think about the action. I just answered it.

"Hello."

"Please don't hang up." The pleading note in his voice tugged at my heart.

"I'm listening," I said softly.

"I know you this is chicken of me but I can't hold back anymore. These past few weeks have been hell. I can't sleep or concentrate. I think about you all the time, Sarah." The words came pouring out of him in a rush, and they could've been my words, my feelings.

"It's killing me not being with you, Sarah." He fell silent for a moment, as if waiting for me to tell him to leave me alone, to hang up, to do something.

"Is that why you called?" I asked. My heart hammered against my ribcage as I waited for his answer.

"Yes." He kept it simple, and that one word thrilled me. "You have no idea what being away from you is doing to me. I love you Sarah."

I thought about how little I'd accomplished, and almost said that I had a pretty good idea.

"Every time I close my eyes, all I can see is you. Your eyes. Your smile. Your body." His voice held a pleading note.

"I need you."

I swallowed hard. How could I say no to that?

Chapter 22

Matthew

I stood by the elevator of my office waiting to go home. What a day. Sarah and I finally spoke. It may have been on the phone but it was a start. Now it was time to go home and sink myself into my wife but I was stopped in my tracks when I reached the building underground car park. Eden stood by my vehicle. What the fuck did he want now.

"Get out of the way Eden" I didn't want to deal with this right now. Sarah was at home waiting for me.

"Poor Matthew, did you have a bad day?"

"Fuck off Eden, I think you have done enough" I grunted before reaching for my car door.

"I think you should listen Matthew, I think you will be very interested in what I have to say. Especially about your little whore" his voice dripping with sarcasm that I wanted to beat out of him.

"What did you call her" I turned rage flowing through my veins.

"You know what happens when you don't share your toys Matthew? They get broken in the fight for them." Eden flicked of what seemed to be an invisible piece of lint from the breast of his tailored jacket.

"What the fuck are you talking about Eden" my voice betraying the control I wanted but couldn't reach.

"I'm talking about you keeping me away from what should be mine, we share remember. We made a promise to each other years ago that we shared. Everything. And if you don't want to share… Well I will just take you little toy away because you've been a bad boy. We wouldn't want Sarah to know all your secrets now would we?"

My head spun. What the game was he playing at. Sarah is my wife not some game.

"What do you want Eden?" my face heating with rage, if this didn't end quickly I may just kill the bastard.

"I want what I always want Matthew, what's yours and you." His voice so matter of fact that was if he expected me to already know the answer.

I lurched forward and grabbed my so-called friend by the collar of his shirt and slammed him against the car.

"Keep your fucking hands off Sarah, if you touch her again"

Eden laughed, why the fuck was he laughing.

"You think I fucked your precious little sub

already" the laughter continued in his voice. "I didn't fuck her. Oh no no no, that's something we do together remember. I did help get rid of that little problem though. I couldn't have something like that come between us. I only share with you Matthew and no pitter patter of little feet will stop me from getting what I want."

I swallowed hard, not even wanting to consider the truth of that last part of his statement. He'd made Sarah miscarry. My child. He'd played me. He knew somehow that I would be there and hear him. He knew what I'd do. I hadn't believed her.

I dropped my hand and stepped back feeling as like all the breath had been kicked out of me.

"Ah, the penny drops"

"What the fuck did you do to her" I rushed at my ex-friend not hesitating to hit him this time. He was ready this time. He wrestled out of the way just as my fist hit the drivers window shatter it. I stepped back my hand marred with blood. Eden stood before me pistol in hand.

"Now, now. Play nice Matthew, you don't want poor little Sarah to have more health problems do you," A sly grin on his face.

"What the do you want Eden?" I ground out.

"Well, Matthew I just want you to be a good boy. So when I tell you, you are going to get into your car and you're going to go home and tell that fuckable little sub of yours nothing. If you do anything to deviate from my plan, the loss of your unborn child will look like child's play." Eden laughed again and shrugged his shoulders. "Too soon"

I had no choice, I had to walk away. If he was able to force my wife to have a miscarriage then he wouldn't think twice on using the gun on me. I got in my car, drove away watching Eden in the review mirror as I left.

I cursed myself. Sarah.

I'd gotten her involved. But it went beyond my believing that she had slept with someone else; I hadn't supported her when she'd told me that she was pregnant, either. Instead, I'd accused her of being pregnant with another man's child. I felt sick, just thinking about the emotional turmoil she had been going through. My job, above everything else, was to protect her. It was to keep her safe. And I was failing.

"My God," I said to myself, and my head as banged my hand against the steering wheel. I bit back the scream that threatened to erupt from my throat. "My God, Matthew, what have you done?"

Chapter 23

Sarah

Matthew had been extremely possessive over the past week. He'd spent every opportunity at home and he'd spent even more time inside of me. It was if he'd been making up for lost time. He'd started talking to me about his childhood years and slowly he had started opening up about his year at Highclere.

Last night he had introduced me to handcuffs. The feeling on hard metal against my wrists. I still wore the faint red line around my wrist this morning. I hadn't bothered covering them as it was a reminder of Matthew. The Matthew, I was only just getting to know.

I had go with him to the office this morning before I was heading off for a book signing at a local book store. We had barely made it to Matthew's floor before he'd started touching me in the elevator.

"Mrs Davidson," he said. "You are looking more beautiful than ever."

"Why thank you, Mr Davidson."

He pulled me to him and kissed me, and I flushed. He unbuttoned the top of my shirt, just a couple of buttons, inspecting the top of my breasts. "You have the most fantastic breast, Mrs Davidson."

He tipped my chin up and kissed me, his tongue rubbing against mine, his stubble raking across my cheeks, his hands roaming my body. He kissed me until I was breathless, senseless, dizzy. It was when backside hit something had that I realised he'd maneuvered us into the conference room.

There was a sound from out in the hallway the ding of the elevator. Jeanette had arrived. Matthew gave me a cocky grin as his hands continued roaming over my ass, apparently not caring that we could be caught. "Matthew," I protested, grabbing at his hand, but his hands continued roaming over my skin, pushing my skirt up.

I could hear the sound of Jeanette's heels clicking against the floor as they came closer. I blushed hot at the thought of her catching me with my skirt up. But Matthew managed to pull it down just as the door to the conference room opened. He was still holding me close, his hand now on my waist, my chest flush with his.

"Oh," Jeanette said when she saw us. Her face, as always, was flawless, her skin poreless and perfect, her hair pulled back in a low bun. She was wearing a grey shift dress and pearls, and she was somehow able to look professional and sexy at the same time.

My blouse and skirt, which had up until a moment ago seemed fine, suddenly felt like I was a kid trying to play dress up.

"I'm sorry, I didn't–"

"It's fine," Matthew said.

"Come in, come in." He kissed me softly on the lips before letting me go, and I blushed at his public display of affection. Jeanette's eyes met mine, and I saw the look of annoyance that flashed there. Her eyes slid down to my open blouse. I followed her gaze to where my top two buttons were undone, and you could see the top of the lace bra Matthew had bought me last week. But not all of it, thank God.

I quickly did the two buttons and pulled at my sleeves, making sure my wrists were covered as they still don the marks from last night. Jeanette gave me look of disgust and I blushed. Matthew kissed me lightly before turning to address Jeanette more directly which I took as my cue to leave before things became more awkward.

Chapter 24

Matthew

Sarah had finally gotten back into her routine of writing after the last couple of months of turmoil. I watched through the doorway as she sat at her computer, headphones on, listening to whatever god awful country music that was bound to be playing. It was usually one of her favourites like Garth Brooks or Keith Urban. She was a sucker for a romantic cowboy. She must have been, she had written over fifteen romance novels about them and the big alpha males that always win the girl. It made me wonder was this our love story. Did I get to keep the girl in the end? I shook my head, I couldn't leave it to chance that I got her in the end.

It had been a typical Saturday night. In fact, it was the first Saturday night in months that we had decided to stay in. I need to get back to the way things use to be and what better than have a few wines and a nice cheese platter.

We started with a bottle of crisp white Sauvignon Blanc and Sarah had barely finished her first glass of Shiraz. Cheese and wine had always been our thing. The cheese platter had had all of my favourites, a beautiful Tasmanian blue, a creamy triple Brie and apricot and almond cheese, topped off with Sarah's favourite Danish salami and line of plain and peppered crackers on each side of the board. We even had our favourite YouTube playlist running on the television in the lounge room as background noise.

Sarah suddenly jumped from the couch and

ran towards the bathroom.

"Baby, are you ok?" I called through the bathroom door. The vomiting noise continued before a flush of the toilet.

"Sarah" but there was no answer. I waited as we weren't the type of couple to share our toileting moments with each other. I passed back down the hall and too the rubbish bin pulling the cheese wrappers to check the used by dates. Made be its the cheese and I hadn't noticed. Nope. All still in date.

We had eaten and drunk the same things so it couldn't be the wine. I poured myself another glass of red.

I heard Sarah's footsteps before I saw here.

"Did you drug me?" Her finger point and her face pink in anger.

"What, how could you…" I didn't even have a chance to reply before the banging on the front door began.

"Police open up "voices flowed through our penthouse apartment.

"Sarah, what the fuck" I turned walking to open the door and sort out what seems to be a huge misunderstanding. Just as I open the door, I hear a thud behind me. Shit. Sarah had collapsed to the floor.

Four police streamed in on rushing to Sarah and another shoving me hard against the wall. As he held me in place I could only watch in horror at my wife unconscious on the lounge room floor.

"Let me go" I begged as paramedics entered.

"The only place you are going Mr Davidson is with us" The officer pushed me against me cuffing my hands behind my back.

"Fuck, Let me go" I yelled struggling against the cuffs. "You have to let me go with my wife."

Chapter 25

Sarah

My head began to pound. The blood rushed through my body, faster and faster, becoming more intense with each beat of my heart. My veins expanded and pulsed, and my temples throbbed. The panic rolled in like a tide, threatening to overtake me, and I forced my mind to move faster in an attempt to stay ahead of it. I felt completely disconnected from my body, like what was happening to me wasn't real.

I ran to the bathroom and vomited. Really,

again. Last time I had been vomiting was the day I miscarried. I knew this time there was no chance that I was pregnant, so maybe its the cheese? It can't be the wine we hadn't drunk that much. I vomited again hearing Matthew checking on me through the closed door. As stood to wash my hands my phone buzzed in my pocket.

Enjoying your night? - number unknown

What the hell, was someone messing with me? My fingers flew across my phone screen in reply.

Who is this? - Sarah Davidson

Your husband isn't everything you thought he was, is he?
Want to know why your sick tonight? Ask

your husband.

- number unknown

I don't know what sick joke you are playing but leave us alone - Sarah

Oh Sarah, I'm only getting just getting started - number unknown

I turned stalking back to the lounge room when another bout of nausea rose in my throat and dizziness plagued me. I spoke but made no sense of the words coming out of my mouth. A pounding banging as if my head was inside of drum began. Everything went black.

"Ma'am, can you hear us" voices broke through the darkness. I tried to respond but the words wouldn't come out.

"Ma'am. Do you know where you are?" the voice said again.

My head lolled from side to side.

"Let me go" my husbands voice made me still. I tried to focus my eyes to where his voice was coming from. As I turned my head a police officer was pushing against my husband who was now cuffed against the wall.

"NO"

"Ma'am please you need to remain calm." The paramedic above me finally came into focus.

Matthew continued to fight against his cuffs before another officer joined then and dragged them out the front door. The Victorian police had taken Matthew away. Taken him away from our inner city penthouse apartment in handcuffs, like a common criminal. He's been arrested.

"No. I need to get up. Please, I need my husband."

Why were they taking my husband. I tried to swing my legs over the side of the stretcher and to hop down but the paramedic put his hands on my shoulders and gently pushed me back down.

Before I knew what I was doing, before I could even think about it, I bit him on the arm. A second later, as if out of nowhere, a team of people surrounded me. Police and paramedics.

"Get me two of lorazapam," someone said. I felt them inject me with something, the sharpness of the needle biting into my arm.

"No," I said.

"No, please! Stop!" I kicked and screamed, but they didn't listen.

I'm one of those crazy people, I thought, stunned. I'm one of those crazy insane people who needs to be knocked out because they can't be trusted not to hurt someone. It was the last thought I remember having before everything went dark.

*****

There were only flashes after that. A nurse placing a blood pressure cuff around my arm.

The prick of an IV. The cool feel of a stethoscope against my neck.

Gradually, everything began fading back in, until I was able to open my eyes and take in my surroundings. I was in a hospital room, and a nurse stood at the side of my bed, checking one of my monitors. She looked over at me, her eyes bright.

"You're awake," she said, sounding pleased.

"Yes." I swallowed and tried to keep myself as calm as possible. The last thing I wanted was to get drugged again.

"Where's my husband?"

"Who?" the nurse asked, her face wrinkling in confusion.

"My husband, Matthew," she chewed her lip.

"I'll go get the doctor," she said. The doctor appeared a few moments later and introduced herself as Dr. Mackenzie. She was tall with her dark shiny hair pinned to the top of her head and what looked to be an undercut underneath.

"How are you feeling, Sarah?" she asked.

"Groggy."

She nodded. "That's from the sedative we gave you. It should be wearing off soon." She grabbed my chart and scanned it. "Do you remember anything from last night?"

"No, where is my husband" my frustration showing

"He was arrested," her voice solemn as if to say she'd seen it all before.

"Arrested ?" I asked through my tears. She sighed.

"Sarah–"

"Please," I said. "Please, I …I need to leave."

She bit her lip, then nodded and gave me a smile.

"Okay, but you have to take it easy. But you have to promise that you won't operate a vehicle."

I shook my head. "I won't."

The taxi took me to the police station, and I walked towards the front entrance, trying not to be intimidated when seeing all of the police cars parked in the lot. Everything about the place screamed authority, and power and as a whole it made me feel small and powerless.

Somehow, just walking inside, I felt guilty, as if she'd committed a crime and was about to be discovered.

I haven't done anything wrong. I'm not guilty of anything and neither is Matthew.

Are you absolutely sure of that? How well do you really know him?

My mind continued spouting arguments and refutations as I continued into the station. There were some chairs and benches, and across the room, a window looking into a back office of some sort. The police don't just arrest people for no reason.

Perhaps I really didn't know my husband as well as I thought I did.

My mouth felt dry, and her heart was

pounding an unsteady rhythm in my chest as she approached the window, behind which a uniformed female officer sat talking on a landline. I waited fidgeting until the officer got off the phone before approaching.

"Hi," she said, uncertainly. The officer was short and squat, with a flat nose and dull brown eyes. "How can I assist you?"

I took a deep breath. "My husband was arrested and brought to this—

"Name," the woman replied, moving to her computer keyboard.

"My name or—"

"His," she interrupted.

"Oh. Matthew. Matthew Davidson."

There was a clacking of the keyboard as the officer's fingers rattled over the keys in rapid-fire fashion.

"He's in Central Booking," the woman informed her.

"I'm sorry, I don't know what—"

"Central Booking is where people go to wait

until they reach bail. Your husband's been arrested, and he'll have to wait like everyone else to see if gets bail." The woman moved away from the computer and picked up a large metal coffee cup. She sipped at it and then started filling out some paperwork, seemingly done with the conversation.

"Ummm… excuse me, ma'am?" I asked softly. The officer didn't turn her head, just kept working. Another person stepped into line behind me and the officer looked up and waved that person forward.

"How can I help you, Sir?" the woman said. I didn't move from the window. "Wait a second, I was here first."

"I answered your question," the woman behind the window said.

"Your husband is awaiting his arraignment. Sometime in the next twenty-four hours, he'll have his time in front of a judge. And if you'll excuse me, I have other people to help."

"That wasn't help," I grumbled my cheeks

flushing.

"How dare you treat me like I'm just some annoying little pest? I'm a person, and my husband's been arrested and I'm frightened."

The officer pursed her lips and took a deep breath.

"Most people who come in here are scared."

"I need to see my husband immediately."

"He's not allowed visitors. If he is released from custody today he will be out in a few hours."

"So I can't even see him?"

"I'm not the arresting officer, so I really don't know what else to tell you." The officer waved forward the man standing behind me again.

Chapter 26

Matthew

As I walked myself into the entry of the station, followed by my very tall and expensive lawyer in a grey suit and a police officer who seemed to be escorting us to the door. When I saw Sarah sitting there, my eyes widened.

"What are you doing?" he said.

"I—I came here to find you," she replied, and then burst into tears. It was humiliating. I couldn't help myself as arms were around her, lifting her to her feet and then hugging her tightly to me.

"Shhh… it's okay. Calm down." Sarah was shaking with relief. She grabbed on tightly to my shirt as she pushed her face into my chest.

"I was so scared…. so, so scared."

"Come outside with me," I told her before turning to the man I had no choice but to trust. My lawyer. "I need to get her out of here."

"That's fine. I can take care of the paperwork. I'll meet you in a few hours." I nodded at my lawyer and walked Sarah outside the station and then brought her to a nearby bench and sat down with her.

"How… how did you get out?" she asked. "Did they drop the charges?" Matthew laughed. "Not quite. I'm free on bail."

Sarah took a deep, shuddering breath in and then let it out, collapsing against Matthew, laying her head on my shoulder.

"I'm so relieved. You have no idea. I was just sitting there, waiting for you to call me." I was silent. I rubbed her back and didn't say anything. Sarah lifted her head and looked at me. I knew my eyes were distant. But I couldn't change how I felt.

"Matthew?" she asked.

I glanced at her. "Yes?"

"They said you were allowed three calls. Why didn't you use one of them to call me?"

I made a grunting noise.

"I was a little preoccupied with trying to get myself out of jail as quickly as possible. And I knew there wasn't anything you'd be able to do to help that happen."

I could see that Sarah felt wounded.

"I'm your wife. Aren't you supposed to call your wife?"

I slid away from her and my body tensed.

"Sarah," my voice a hiss of impatience. I lowered my head and ran my hands through my thick hair.

"I really can't do this right now."

"Do what?"

"Sit here and justify everything I did after I got arrested." I sat straight up and turned my head to stare at her. My eyes were burning bright with frustration.

"I was just arrested because someone made an anonymous photo call saying that I drugged and abused my wife."

She looked away from him and her tears seemed to instantly vanish.

"What," she said. "That wasn't me, Matthew."

Sarah got up and started to walk away from me, shaking her head. I jumped to his feet and caught her, grabbing her wrist.

"Stop. Stop it right now."

Sarah turned to face me.

"What happened last night Matthew?" her voice small like a child asking for something she knew she wasn't allowed to have.

"You that's what happened last night"

"Why are you so cruel to me?" I knew that my face was a mask that she couldn't penetrate.

"I'm tired," I said.

"So am I, Matthew," she said, her voice cracked.

I sighed. "I will talk to my lawyer in a few hours and discuss the charges."

"No, You're going to beat the charges because you're innocent." Her voice more confident then he'd heard in a while.

"What makes you think I'm as innocent as you claim me to be."

"Because Matthew, I know you'd never hurt me. Ever."

Chapter 27

Sarah

We arrived back at home and not spoken much. Matthew had announced his intention to take a long, hot shower, and then disappeared. I sat down and tried to watch some television, but found it hard to focus on anything. She kept replaying moments from the last. Remembering the moment I had woken up in the hospital alone and fuzzy moments the police had stormed into our home when Matthew had been placed in handcuffs and told that he was being arrested.

The truth was I had no idea what had happened in the last twenty-four hours. The only thing I did now what that I am exhausted, but I don't want to close my eyes. Matthew wouldn't have hurt me… He is the most loving, supportive and caring man I have ever met. I know he loves me.

Matthew finally emerged downstairs in sweatpants and a white t-shirt, looking refreshed from his shower. Every time I saw him, I was still struck by how ferociously gorgeous the man was. His dark hair was still damp from the shower, the fringe hanging over his forehead. My gaze moved to his strong jaw, those cobalt blue eyes, and then she took in the tight, toned body that was tantalisingly within reach as he came towards me.

"You look tired," he said.

"I'm am," I admitted.

"Do you want to go to sleep?"

"Sure, if you are ready." My reply not exactly a question but more of a statement to see if Matthew had planned to sleep next to me in our bed tonight.

As I enter our bedroom Matthew's arms surround me and his mouth hot on my neck. His licks hot lashes sending shivers of pleasure through my body.

Warning bells go off in my head. I need to take control of this situation. I need to get answers not get seduced by my husband. But his tongue brushes against my neck again, and all of my protests slip out of my head. Certainly there's nothing wrong with teasing him a little, letting him think I've succumbed to his charms. I'll give him a taste, fuel his desire, and then I'll have him right where I want him. He tightens his hold on my hip, pulling me closer to him. His other hand moves to the shoulder of my shirt, yanking it aside so he can continue his soft march of kisses. I shiver involuntarily.

"Matthew," I whisper.

"Perhaps we should—" I gasp as he nips at

me with his teeth.

"Is that what you really want?" he says against my skin. His hand moves forward along the neckline of my shirt, his fingers skimming just beneath the edge of the fabric. He slides the garment off my shoulder, exposing the top curve of my breast.

"You have such beautiful breasts Sarah," he says, his mouth against my ear once more. His hand moves lower, gliding over one of my breasts and then the other, his touch featherlight. My breathing is shallow, uneven. I know I should stop him, take back control of the situation, but I don't. In this moment I'm not even sure I want to.

"Feel the frustration building?" he breathes against my ear.

His hand moves lower and lower, with such agonising slowness that I have to struggle to keep from pressing back against him. His fingers graze my nipple. I stiffen as he takes the nub and rolls it gently between his forefinger and thumb.

"It's subtle at first," he whispers, giving a soft pull.

"Your blood pumping faster, your skin becoming more sensitive. The beginning of an ache between your legs." His fingers become more insistent, pinching and tugging at my nipple.

"That's where we want to focus. On that ache." I close my eyes and let my head roll back against his shoulder. My nipple is rock hard beneath his touch, and still he massages it, pulling and twisting to the point of pain. I should tell him to stop, but I don't.

And then, suddenly, his fingers release me. A sound of protest escapes me before I can stop it, and Matthew chuckles into my hair.

"We're not done yet," he says. He moves to the other breast, pulling it halfway out of the shirt so that he can reach the nipple. He repeats his rolling and pulling until that one, too, is hard and sensitive against his rougher skin. "It builds slowly," he murmurs into my hair.

"But little by the little the ache grows stronger, more insistent."

He moves his hand from my hip and across my upper thigh, stopping at the place where my legs meet. He pushes down softly, just enough to press the fabric of the skirt against my most sensitive spot.

"What, then, is the cause of this frustration?" he breathes.

His hand slides further between my legs. I push back against him involuntarily, and he tightens his grip on me, keeping me hard against him. I know that I need to stop him. I need to pull away. I need to control this situation. I need answers.

"Matthew… Stop" my voice is breathy.

"Oh Sarah, just give me this. Please."

"Matthew, I need…" my words are cut off.

"So wet already," he whispers in my ear. His hand moves slowly—too slowly. I squirm against him.

This is a bad idea, a tiny voice in my head reminds me. Stop him. Push him away. You're supposed to be the one in control. You're supposed to get answers.

With all my strength, I push away from him. I have too.

"Matthew… I can't"

Chapter 28

Matthew

I knew that Sarah wanted answers but I had nothing. I didn't know. All I knew is that right now I needed her. I needed her naked and under me. My frustration grew.

Chapter 29

Sarah

"Dammit, Sarah , don't leave me hanging," he says.

"I'm not leaving you hanging I need to know what the hell happened last night. Where the hell did the police come from and how did I end up in the hospital?" But it's when he reaches for me again that really ticks me off.

"What the fuck is going on? Fuck this! I'm not your fucking puppet! You can't just expect me to have all this shit happen and not as questions."

"Look, Sarah, I'm sorry," Matthew said sounding defeated.

"You just drive me crazy, you know that? Please. Please. I promise answer anything you want just come to bed with me. I need you."

I'm having trouble standing still, so I grab Matthew's shirt from the ground and slip it on. I march over to the table, grab our half-finished bottle of wine from dinner, and head over to the glass sliding doors at the far side of the dining room. I don't care that it's raining. I pull open the doors and step out onto the balcony. We were on the eightieth floor of the Eureka tower in Melbourne.

The cold, wet air is a welcome slap in the face. A welcome relief. The rain has slowed to a drizzle and wind howled around me. I lean against the railing and take a swig of wine right from the bottle.

I didn't care if it wasn't ladylike as my mother would have said. My life is a mess, and I'm not sure what to do anymore. Did Matthew do this, did I? What wasn't he telling me? Could I still trust the man I married. Or was this my doing? Did I get my husband arrested?

I take another swig and stare out across the city lights still visible through the drizzle. How did life get so fucked up.

"Drinking without me?" Matthew's voice snaps me out of my thoughts.

He holds out his hand for the wine bottle, and I pass it over. He takes a drink and hands it back. "Sarah, I would never hurt you. You have to know that. I love you more than my next breath. As for what happened last night…" Matthew sighed. "I have no idea what happened….."

"But you must, it was just us here" I pleaded.

"It was just us, that's what I don't understand. One minute we were enjoying some wine, cheese and music. Then you were in the bathroom vomiting. "

"But we hadn't drunk much" my voice

sounding as confused as I felt.

"Exactly, that's what I can't work out. One minute all was fine and the next you accused me of spiking your drink and you were vomiting." Matthew voice was strained like the memories of my accusation had truly hurt him.

"I don't get it, why would I say that." I stepped forward raising my hand to touch Matthew.

"I don't know, but you did." Matthew shrugged.

I stepped forward wrapping my arms around him. "Oh, Matthew. I'm sorry. I'm so sorry. I know you'd never do that to me."

Chapter 30

Matthew

I had been in and out of meetings with investors for a new seventy story project in their city offices when my phone dinged. I swiped the message open. Eden. It had been weeks since the underground car park incident and weeks since his threats about Sarah.

I have a little present for you, it will be just like old times - E

I immediately tried to call Sarah. Fuck, no

answer. I dialled again. Still no answer. My heart raced. Why isn't she picking up.

What have you done to her? - M

Why don't you come and see. She ready and waiting like a good girl? - E

Tell me where she is - M

I raced home continuing to call Sarah's phone. As I arrived I searched apartment. Nothing.

Tell me where the fuck my wife is - M

Oh, Matthew you should know by now I always come to you. We are just catching on lost time. - E

* * *

The next thing I received is a video file. That's where I knew this deadly game Eden was playing had to stop and now.

"Matthew, please, please save us" Jeanette's frantic scream on the screen in front of me, sent chills through me. She'd been tied up. She said us. Eden must have Sarah too. Why, Jeanette. She is just my secretary. I replayed the video looking for clues to where they were. The scene panned across Jeanette again. The logo. Shit my logo. My office.

I called triple 000. I knew this wasn't something that was going to turn out well. Not after my last run in with Eden.

I couldn't take any chances. Sarah and Jeanette were in trouble.

"What the hell is going on?" I muttered under my breath as I looked up from the service elevator from the car park and saw nothing. I crossed the marble flooring. The building looked empty. Why wasn't security at the front desk.

Walked down the hall I could hear Eden

before I saw him.

"YOU BITCH," he yelled.

Chapter 31

Sarah

I'd come to see if Matthew had wanted to go for lunch after everything we'd been through and then last night. That's when I heard the voices. Yelling coming from his office.

The door was slightly ajar and I could see Matthew from where I was standing. I recognised the other voice.

Eden.

I cracked the door to intervene. Matthew shook his head letting me know that it wasn't safe. I dial 000 as I shut the door and waited for the police to arrive and stop this madness. As the argument got more heated, I heard the rise and fall of angry voices and then silence. That worried me. I cracked the door and saw Matthew laying face down on the wooden floor as Eden pulled Jeanette off the office chair and positioned her next to Matthew.

"I know you're out there, Sarah!" Eden called from Matthew's office. I quietly closed the door and placed the Jeanette's reception chair under the handle, trying to figure out what to do next.

"Sarah, why don't you come in here an join us. Don't you want to know why Matthew has been such a bad boy?" he yelled.

"Let them go," I called back as I looked around the room for a possible weapon before yelling, "Why Eden, Why are you doing this?"

"Sarah, Sarah, Sarah. Our dear Mathew here just doesn't like to share his new toy."

Shit Eden's talking about me. He wants to share me. God, what do I do? Keep him talking the longer he talks the more likely help will come.

"Why is sharing me, so important to you?"

"Oh sweetheart, I don't merely want to share. I want him. He was always supposed to be mine. But no a little whore like you caught his eye," he said startling me as he threw himself against the door and shoved it open enough to get the hand holding the gun pointed straight at me.

"I don't have anything to lose anymore, Sarah. You're going to pay for you taking what was mine."

"Eden, none of this makes any sense," I said as I moved toward the corner where he couldn't see me, thinking that if he started shooting at least I'd have some chance of avoiding the bullets.

"It doesn't matter," he growled. "Nothing matters anymore."

"So, you're going to kill us all because Matthew wouldn't have sex with you. Because he wouldn't share?" I asked as I searched for a way to keep him talking. " Why did you come to us, why didn't you just ask."

"Shut the fuck up," Eden growled again. "I deserved to have him, after all the years of playing second fiddle to all the whores and subs he used."

"I'm not his sub, " my voice flat .

"You have no clue do you, he might have come off all sweet and romantic but he has needs. Needs you will never fill. I could have made him happy but no. You got your claws into him and just had to fix him didn't you," he said as I watched his arm slide down the door frame.

Suddenly, on the other side of the door, I heard a loud bang and then saw Eden pull the gun out of the crack between the door and the frame. I heard a loud thud and then two voices shouting in the hallway. I stayed crouched in the space between the wall and the door frame as the gun went off. I heard another thud, and then a voice broke the silence that followed.

"He's dead, but you going to take his place. You're going to be my little bitch and do exactly as I say or you'll have a bullet in you just like Matthew," Eden said quietly. His voice sent a chill up my spine.

"Don't do it! Don't do it!" Jeanette screamed from Matthew's office. I knew I had one chance to stop this deadly plan and, that either way, I had a pretty good chance of dying. I decided it was better to have it over with quickly rather than having to suffer.

So, I yanked open the door and ran towards Eden where he stood with a knife in one hand and the gun in the other. I raced toward him with my eye on the gun from his hand.

Halfway there, I heard a loud crack as the frosted glass of office door shattered and Eden slumped to the ground.

Bewildered, I looked around trying to figure out what had just happened. Eden rose up with the gun in his hand and pointed it at me. I screamed as the second shot hit him and he fell over dropping the gun to the floor. I kicked it out of the way and ran to Jeanette who was crying hysterically in a pool of shattered glass. She'd been cut, but as I untied the ropes that bound her.

"He shot him!" she cried as she pointed towards the conference room that back onto Matthews office. I ran around to the doorway and saw Matthew lying in a pool of blood on the wooden floor. He wasn't moving. I dropped to my knees and searched for a pulse, and then lifted him up to find that the bullet had gone into his abdomen.

"Matthew, please no, god no"

I pulled at his shirt trying to ebb the flow of blood. It pulse through my hand as I held it firm.

"Jeanette, get help! Go get help!" I shouted as I pressed his shirt into the wound.

"They're already here," she replied weakly as a team of Victorian police officers slammed open the door and rushed inside the clubs private room with their guns drawn.

"Don't shoot! Don't shoot!" Jeanette screamed as they aimed their guns at her.

"Please, he needs help, he's hurt." One of the policemen rushed to Eden, the other ran to Matthew.

"Please," I pleaded, hearing the desperation in my own voice. "Please, you need to help him." The officer spoke into his walkie talkie.

"We need a paramedics down here, immediately. White male with severe gunshot."

He looked at me. "Are you okay, ma'am?"

"Please, he's dying. You have to help him, you need to do CPR or something on him, please, he needs help." The policeman looked at me, his eyes filled with sympathy.

"HELP HIM!" I screamed. Matthew wasn't moving.

The world started to spin as paramedics rushed into the room and began to work frantically on Matthew, pumping his chest.

"He's dead," I cried. "He's dead, isn't he?" But no one would answer me. The paramedics were working on Matthew, their hands moving in tandem as they tried to force life back into his body. I watched as one of them breathed into Matthew's mouth while the other one performed chest compressions, their movements perfectly choreographed.

"Ma'am, you need to come with me," the policeman who'd called for help said. "We need to get you out of here. You need medical attention." He had salt and pepper hair and a broad chest. His face was weathered, but his eyes were kind. The combination made me think he'd been around for a long time and seen a lot, that he'd been faced with the unthinkable.

"I can't leave him," I said. "I need to know

if he's going to be okay." I was starting to get hysterical–I could hear it in my voice.

"You need to come with me so we can get you looked at," the officer said before he put his hand gently on my elbow, and began leading me to the door.

I shook him off. "No,"

"No, I need to make sure he's okay."

"We have a pulse," one of the paramedics tending to Matthew said. I gasped in relief and began to cry, the sobs racking my body. But a second later, they brought in a stretcher and lifted Matthew onto it. His body was still lifeless, and the paramedic who'd announced Matthew's had a pulse jumped onto the stretcher and continued giving him chest compressions.

I felt like I could feel him slipping away. He'd been so pale, and there'd been so much blood.

If they'd found a pulse, why were they still doing CPR?

I started to follow the stretcher, but the policeman stepped in front of me. "Ma'am," he said. "Please, ma'am, you need to get checked out."

"I'm going with him." I pleaded.

"You can't go with him. There won't be any room in the ambulance."

A second set of paramedics loaded Eden onto a stretcher as Jeanette and I were taken down to the second ambulance. Meanwhile, the police secured the office and began their investigation.

A female paramedic stepped in front of me."We're going to take you to the hospital to get checked out," the paramedic said.

She helped Jeanette and I up into the ambulance before closing the doors and taking off for the hospital. I held Jeanette's hand the whole ride to the hospital hoping that Matthew was still alive. Suddenly the fact that he'd lied and called me whore didn't matter. I love him and I can't bear to lose him.

Chapter 32

Jeanette

I knew she would think I was the victim, the stupid bitch. God, she even held my hand like I was some lost little girl. Yuck. I wasn't held captive, I was there to have things back the way they use to be. Me between Matthew and Eden. The way things should have been since they took my virginity. Me between the men I loved.

I had been a college freshman, when I met them. I'd been working at gala event as a waitress and tripped on the stairs with a tray full of glasses. If it hadn't of been for Matthew I would have broken them all. He'd caught me and the tray sandwiching me between him and Eden. His words still fresh in my memory.

"Looks like we caught a one E, between us like all good girls should be." Remember drinking in his broad shoulders, dark hair and husky voice just like a aged whiskey. His warmth flushing through me. It was the man called E drew her a step back, until their bodies aligned and I could feel his hard, thick, substantial erection pressing insistently against my bottom. I closed her eyes as a rush of moisture dampened my panties and my sex pulsed. I swallowed back a groan, struggling against the shameless urge to bend over, spread her legs, and beg him to fill her, take her.

"Are you okay there sweetheart, my big friend here, didn't scare you did he?" His voice full of laughter.

I wasn't scared no, it was a need of desire that ran through me.

"Ha, no I'm more scared to lose this job then I am of you two." I forced myself to take the sarcastic tone like a shield to protect my true feelings.

"Did you hear that Matthew, not scared. That sounds like a challenge to me" E's breath hot against my ear.

I started to pull away and they let me go. "Um, thank you for saving me from falling. "

"It was our pleasure, I believe I will take that drink now though. How about you Eden?"

"I think I will, the gala may just be worth staying for after all."

That night was the first night Matthew and Eden had shared me. It was the night I fell in love with two men. But that bitch came along and fucked everything up.

Eden had been the one to come up with the plan, he was the one to pay for the cosmetic surgery. I love my new look. New nose, chin and boobs sent guys wild. Matthew never seemed to notice though in the six months I had worked for him. I bit the inside of my lip just as I did anytime I got upset. I will not give them the satisfaction of crying. No. I can't cry, it would mean I'm weak. I'm not going to let them get away with it. Matthew is mine and I'm going to take him back.

I still can't believe that they didn't notice it

was me that put the abortion drugs into Sarah's coffee, just like Eden had planned. It was supposed to be the straw that broke the camels back so to speak. It should have been the end of their marriage especially after we set up the scene at Highclere to make it sound like Eden had slept with Sarah. But no, the bitch still said she loved him. Well it's time to put an end to that. Let's see how much she loves him after I'm finished with him.

The End of

Married Games

Revenge Games

This page is intentionally left blank

Chapter 1

Matthew

"Oh shit," I groaned as I rose up through the layers of drug-induced sleep as pain flares through me.

"Fuck that hurts!"

"Shh, shh, lay still," the voice said moved around the room. I couldn't tell who it was because my eyes felt like they were glued shut and it took an enormous amount of effort to crack them open. When I did, everything was fuzzy, but I could feel a hand holding mine.

"What the hell happened?" I mumbled through cracked dry lips.

"You were shot," the voice said.

"How long have I been out?" I asked as I tried

again to open my eyes and focus on my surroundings.

"Where am I?"

"You're in Monash Hospital in the ICU," the voice replied.

"You've been out for three days and we were beginning to really worry."

"Eh, I'm fine," I said as I struggled to try and move my arms. I wanted to sit up. I wanted to open my eyes and see what was going on around me. I wanted to know whose voice that was.

"No, no, no," the voice said gently holding my shoulder to the mattress. "You are not in any shape to be getting up, Mr. Davidson."

"Sarah, I need to find Sarah," I said suddenly remembering the events that had led to this point.

"Where is Sarah?"

"I'm right here, Matthew," Sarah whispered in my ear as she squeezed my hand. I opened my eyes and focused them on the face next to me. Her blue eyes were bright with tears as she gripped my hand more tightly and smiled.

"I'm right here. I'm not going anywhere."

"Oh, thank God, you're okay," I sighed as I felt the pain in my side begin to throb intensely. I groaned as Sarah tucked the button that released pain medication in my other hand and said, "Press it when you're in pain, it'll ease it."

I pressed the button and a few minutes later, I felt the pain begin to ease as I fell back into a groggy, half-wakeful state. I could feel Sarah's hand tucked in mine as I drifted back to sleep.

Chapter 2

Sarah

It had been two weeks since Matthew had been released from hospital. The police had been by and taken statements from Matthew, Jeanette and myself. I still couldn't believe that Eden had tried to kill us all. Most of all that it was all because he was in love with Matthew.

I had tried to be as attentive as I could. Making sure he rested and even disconnecting the home phone when the his office continued to call over and over again.

Jeanette his assistant had been amazing. She had managed his schedule and put off anything that wasn't urgent. Tomorrow though Matthew was supposed to return to work. Matthew didn't seem phased at all about it but something still felt off. I just couldn't put my finger on what it was. I was just glad that Jeanette would be there to take care of Matthew when I couldn't. I would never of thought that I might actually want to become friends with the woman but it was almost impossible she was just so, nice. She had come by daily to check on us both and to the hospital too. She'd helped with the police and the hospital making arrangements for all the little things I hadn't even thought of and when Matthew finally came home she arranged everything. She had been a god sent really.

Matthew and I hadn't gotten back to normal yet. I still wasn't one hundred percent sure what had gone on at Matthews office but Eden was dead. The police said they weren't pressing charges but I still didn't know who against. Did Matthew shoot him or did Jeanette?

Chapter 3

Jeanette

Jealousy….
It's a poisonous feeling.
One that grows and grows,
wraps itself around your heart
and takes over your soul.

Autumn came and went as quickly as a leaf falling from its branch, and winter took hold, sending a chill through Melbourne, freezing what was old to make room for the new.

He's inside me, taking over me, consuming me,

hypnotising my thoughts, claiming my body as his. I moan his name, and my fingers dig into his back as he pushes rhythmically inside me. He plays me as if I'm his favorite instrument, and I make every sound before I crescendo. This is when he's mine, when I'm the only thing in his thoughts, where time outside of us doesn't matter.

He grabs my wrists and pins them down—it's a rule I break often.

No marks.

I can't mark him, but he marks me.

"Matthew ," I moan.

The tension between my thighs builds, ready to throw itself off the cliff that is us. I rock beneath him. His body is hard and his skin wet. His eyes look into mine. That's become one of my favorite parts, when he not only gives me his body but shares his soul. His clear blue eyes clouded with lust, with need. He needs me. I free him. This is when he's alive. I can feel him coming close.

"Don't stop. I'm almost there," I plead, begging him to keep going, to not stop or pull away.

He moves faster and faster, granting my request, and his lips kiss mine, taking them in a slow, passionate kiss I usually don't get from him but I give him all the time. It's so natural, so wonderful, but he usually keeps it from me. This kiss, even if his words never say it, lets me know how he feels, what he can't say , and it's what pushes me over the edge, relieving all my tension. My toes curl, and my eyes roll to the back of my head. I pant to catch my breath, and my body quivers before he follows.

His body rests on mine, our breathing frantic, our hearts beating rapidly but as one. My fingers trail up his back, and I kiss his shoulder. He rolls off me, catches his breath, and pulls me against his naked body. I revel in the small amount of time we have, the moments when he's guilt-free, when I pretend that it's just us with no complications. I pretend my heart isn't going to break the moment he leaves, that reality doesn't end the best part of my world.

Those moments, that small window when he's like this, are short, and when he removes his arm from across my stomach, I know it's over. The bed shifts, and he gets out of bed and grabs his clothes. His body is beautiful, sculpted and hard, and I feel lucky that he shares it with me.

His eyes find mine. I try to smile even though I

want to cry. I hate this part. He knows I do, and I don't want to ruin what just happened, but I know the words I'm going to speak will. I can't hold them in anymore, so I try to prolong the time by trying not to say them. I try to think of everything else to say.

Beep, beep, beep….Good Morning is six am and now for the morning traffic update in beautiful Melbourne!

I pick up my pillow and throw it at my alarm clock. Today Matthew would be back at the office. Today would be the start of getting back what belongs to me.

Matthew.

Chapter 4

Matthew

I watched as Jeanette fussed about me as I entered the office. Time had certainly changed things, Eden had changed everything. It is was my first day back at work since the day I had been shot only meters away. The blood stains were gone but the memories remain. A shudder ran through me as I struggled to tear my eyes away from the spot in my office. Would the feeling fade? Maybe I should move the office to a new building. One without so many memories.

"Matthew, are you okay?" Jeanette's voice pulling me from my hypnagogic hallucination.

"Oh, Sorry what did you say?" Jeanette turned

looking at the place I couldn't seem to stop staring at. Rounding my desk she placed her hand to my shoulder.

"Matthew, I'm here for you. If its too much I can reschedule all your meetings. You don't have to be here," her voice held no pity just a comfort I hadn't felt before with Jeanette.

"It's fine, maybe we should look at a new office space."

"This office certainly had many memories, but not all bad. I loved this place from my first day."

Jeanette's first day. So naive, so innocent.

One year earlier...

As splinters of the frame crashed all over the hardwood, he took a deep breath, attempting to rein in my anger.

"Don't move," I ordered.

"I... I was just looking for," she stammered and bent over to pick up a shard of glass. "I'm so sorry. It's just that I... I needed information and you weren't..."

"I sent you the files," I began. As I approached, I felt a crunch under my heel.

"I'll clean this up." Her eyes went wide.

"Don't. Just leave it."

"No, it will only take a second," Jeanette insisted. Crouched over, she carefully placed a jagged remnant into her palm.

"Jeanette, just stop."

As she lifted her eyes to meet mine, my anger turned to sympathy. Instinct drove me as much as facts. Soon enough, I'd question her, and she'd either be fired or still working for him. My eyes flickered to the soft cleavage peeking through her blouse, and I struggled to stay on task. God, I hadn't worked this closely with a woman for years and this was why. Unsure of whether she'd detected my momentary lapse of focus, I forced an impassive mask across my face.

"I'm sorry. It's just… the meeting tomorrow… I was…"

She reached down, shifting her focus from my eyes to the floor and back again. Her lips trembled as her hand touched the picture frame.

"Just leave it."

"I'll clean it up." A small smudge of blood stained the dark wood.

"Do. Not. Move," I commanded, taking sight of what she'd done to her hand. Surprised she hadn't flinched, I surmised the slice of the glass hadn't registered. I'd cut himself enough times to know that the pain didn't always set in until you saw the injury.

"But I... oh my God," Jeanette said as she realised what she'd done. The broken fragment fell to the ground as she gripped her wrist.

Without asking, I scooped Jeanette up into my arms, and kicked open the door. I tried not to allow her citrus-scented hair to distract him as I made my way to my office. It was difficult to tame the twitch of my dick as her soft body brushed against mine. I knew it was off limits to go there. Not only were they in the office, she was injured and I am married.

Get it the fuck together, I thought. I eyed my bathroom. Squeezing through the entrance, I gently placed her on the counter, taking note of the small pieces of glass that sparkled from her shoes and stockings. Without giving a thought to what to do next, I stripped off my shirt and knelt down, my eyes meeting hers.

Although she wasn't crying, he could see the tears readying to fall.

"You're going to be all right, sweetheart. Just give me your hand."

"I'll be fine. Please, no."

"We need to get it under some water, stop the bleeding. We have to make sure we get all the glass out."

She extended her hand to me, and licked her lips, tensing as if expecting more pain. I took a quick look at the cut. I tested the water temperature before running both their hands under the stream.

"This might sting a little."

"Ow. Dammit, I can't believe I just did that." She attempted to tear her hand away, but I held her firm.

"You're not going anywhere, now. I warned you it was going to sting." I raised an eyebrow at her until she stopped moving. Hearing her speak frankly was surprising but refreshing. Cursing could make even the worst agony seem tolerable. I'd known there was fire underneath the woman who'd negotiated the contract in my office.

"I'm sorry." She gave a small laugh, a rosy hue flushing her cheeks.

"Almost done. Now listen, Janette. You don't seem to take directions very well so far, so I'm going to remind you that while you're here, I'm the boss. That means, when I talk, you listen."

"But…" she began.

"No talking. This is my company, my office." I shushed firmly.

"This is serious. The things we do here, which I'll get to in a moment, are sometimes highly confidential

government contracts. Deadly, to certain departments if they get into the wrong hands."

I saw the flicker of fear in her eyes. I'd never intentionally set out to intimidate her, but the reality of my life was paramount. I constructed top secret government facilities, no even the men working on construction knew what they were for. It was always a need to know basis and they didn't need to know.

With her free hand, she wiped a tear, looking away from me. She took a deep breath, and returned my gaze.

The emotion I saw inside her caused a stir of arousal. Goddammit, of all the times to get this reaction, this was not it. Confused by my attraction, I focused my effort on cleaning her hand.

"It looks like the bleeding has slowed. Just keep it under the water a second while I get a towel."

As I slowly released her wrist, he noted that she never took her eyes off me. Yet she submitted to my request… this time. No fighting or arguing. I couldn't be certain if she was acquiescing because I'd scolded her or if she truly understood I'd meant what I'd said.

Matthew slid open a cabinet drawer and retrieved a clean washcloth. After turning off the spigot, I wrapped the fabric around her hand, keeping pressure on the wound. I opened the bathroom closet door, and began to rummage through, in search of a Band-Aid. As I glanced back toward Jeanette, I noticed the look of shock on her face.

"You have a lot of injuries around here?" she asked, her eyes wide.

"Yes. No. Oh hell, okay, yeah, sometimes. Look, Jeanette, we really need to talk," I hedged. I knew my bathroom supplies made it look as if I was stocking an ambulance. Accidents happened. Granted, usually not on the executive floor, but I liked to be prepared. And out on the construction site, I was more likely to play down an injury than run to get first aid in front of co-workers. Jeanette diverted her eyes, bringing her hand to her chest. The bright red stain on her shirt had begun to crust over into a deep shade of brown.

"Your hand should be all right." I smiled as I set the butterfly bandage into place.

"The patient will live. This time."

"Thank you," she said, shifting on the counter.

"Where do you think you're going?" I asked, placing my palms onto her knees.

"Um, out of the bathroom, I guess."

"No."

"No?"

"Nylons in Melbourne summer?" I asked.

"I'm sorry, what?"

"You may be a transplant but I didn't think these," I tugged at her stockings, "were very comfortable. But you know what's even more troubling?"

"What? No wait, how come you know so much about what women wear on their legs?"

"Many reasons." I smiled.

"But I think I'll go with business. Yeah, that sounds good."

"Business?"

"Fabrics. Plastics. Metals. Some materials, you want them hard, impenetrable. Others," I brushed the back of my fingers softly against her cheek, catching a stray hair that had come loose from her bun. My eyes fell to her soft lips and then met hers.

"They're designed to be soft but strong." She smiled, silently watching me.

"And these," I pinched a stretchy section off her thigh and let it snap back into place, "hold particles. Like glass."

"Oh," she replied softly.

"I don't think… well, I don't feel a cut or anything."

"Let me have your shoes." Before she could protest, I inspected her stilettos. I carefully removed each one and shook it over the trash bin. A ping resounded as pellets rained into the tin container. I set them on the toilet seat and then evaluated my next move.

With her soft pink lips within inches, I yearned to touch Jeanette, and not just a little bit. I briefly closed my eyes, and my recurrent fantasy flashed through my mind, of her bent over, while he slammed inside of her. I fought a smile. Before shaking it off, I'm married.

"Is something funny?" I heard her ask and my gaze beamed up to hers.

"No, not funny. Something to look forward to, perhaps."

"What?"

"About these." I ignored her question and glanced to her legs. "They need to come off."

"What did you say?"

"I think you heard me quite clearly. And since you aren't going to be able to get them off without the tiny bits of glass digging into your skin, the question is, 'How should we get these torturous things off of you?'"

"Do you really think that's necessary? Maybe if I lift up you could help me pull them off?" She raised her legs, and several tiny fragments reflected under the light.

"Well, fuck. What am I supposed to do?"

"Fuck? Hmm, that may be an option later but let's

get these off first, shall we?"

"No, I just was saying…" she stammered.

"I'm teasing you." I paused. "Maybe. Let me ask you a question, Jeanette."

"Yes?"

"Do you trust me?" I smiled as the idea came to him. She couldn't possibly trust him yet, but oh, how she would learn.

"Umm, I suppose"

"Do you want to close your eyes or open them?"

"What are you talking about?"

"Now don't shoot down this idea because I actually think it may be the best solution… all things considered."

"What is it? Just get them off." I turned my back and selected my instrument. Holding it up, I gave her a smile, hoping it'd take the sting out of my suggestion.

"Scissors? Are you kidding me?"

"Not in the least."

"No way."

With a small chuckle, "Way. They're bandage scissors. We can start at your waist and slide straight down to your toes. They'll peel right off without scratching your skin."

"Oh my God. I seriously don't believe this."

"Think of it as penance for going into my office."

"About that..."

"Yes, about that." Figuring it was as good a time as any, I pressed her for answers.

"Why were you in my office?"

"In my defense, I told you I needed your laptop. There was something in the files you sent me. Tomorrow's meeting and I didn't want to be unprepared."

"So you broke into my office... the first day you come to work for me?"

"I was going to ask you if I could have it, but you didn't give me your mobile phone number. I knocked on your door. You weren't there."

"I saw you," I replied, toying with the shiny metal instrument.

"You saw me?" She rolled her eyes and set them back on me.

"The cameras?"

"Yes, the cameras. I see everything. You want to tell me why it couldn't wait until tomorrow?"

"There was no guarantee I'd see you before the meeting. You may not mind walking in cold to a meeting, but that's not how I roll," she challenged.

"I see," I laughed.

"Not how you roll, you say. I'm going to be setting some ground rules before you end up out the door."

"Ground rules?"

"See, you do listen." I smiled and held up tI scissors.

"Let's table this, shall we? It appears we have more pressing business at hand."

"Do you know what you're doing with those things? I probably could just scoot up." She tugged her shirt out of her skirt and wriggled on the counter.

"Hey, if you want to take off your clothes, then well, who am I to stop you, but I think if you just let me reach up…"

"Okay." She sighed.

"I'll hold out the waistband and you snip it. Agreed?"

"It'll be painless." For you. As soon as I put my hands on her, it would be a race in time to control my growing erection.

"Promise?" She gave me a small smile and lifted the side of her skirt so I could reach underneath.

"You must learn to trust me, Jeanette. Easy now," I instructed. My fingers worked quickly as I felt my way up her thigh to where she held the band taut. With a snip, I worked backward, cutting a line down to her toe.

"Now the other side. Don't move. When I'm

finished, I'm going to lift you out of here, get you away from all this glass."

My cock jerked as my wrist brushed over her leg. Clipping away, it only took him seconds to make my way down to her other foot. When I was finished, I placed the scissors on the counter. A pause of silence passed between them as my eyes met hers. Never shifting my gaze, I slipped my hands under her skirt. The warmth of her pussy heated my palms as I gripped the band, pulling it toward the ground. Sating my need to touch her, the tips of my fingers met her skin, carefully brushing the fabric aside.

She willingly spread her legs, allowing him to drape the nylon away from her skin. Freeing her toes, I stood up, the sides of my abdomen grazing her inner thighs.

"Put your arms around my neck," I instructed. Without questioning him, she did as told, and he shivered in anticipation of what I could do with her once they were out of the bathroom.

"You ready?" I asked, my voice low. I wasn't sure whether or not I was asking to move her, kiss her, or fuck her. my balls tightened and damn, if my brain didn't kick him right back in the nuts. Get her to the sofa and stop fooling around, Jesus Christ.

"Yes," she breathed. She licked her lips.

"Wait. Ready for what?"

"This," I responded, picking her up off the counter in one smooth action. I reached under her skirt, cupping her bottom, and plucked the offending stockings off, throwing them to the ground. I grunted as she wrapped her legs around him, the warmth of her core skimming against my abs.

I wasted no time getting out of the bathroom, depositing her gently onto my sofa. The sound of her soft gasp took him by surprise and I forced himself to remove my hands from her waist. Not wanting her to see the expression of desire on my face, I turned back toward the bathroom, kicking my boots off. A glutton for punishment, I returned to her side. Kneeling down on the floor, he checked her legs for glass.

"Let me see." As I ran my palms down her thighs, inspecting her calves and feet, she squeezed her legs tight together. I glanced up to her flushed face and knew instantly she was every bit as aroused as I was. She nervously tugged at her shirt.

"You look good. I mean," I coughed, "no cuts. Do you feel any pain? Anything?"

"No, I'm fine, thanks. I feel like an idiot for making such a God-awful mess, but I think my ego will survive. Thank you, Mr.…"

"Matthew. I think we're beyond formalities now, don't you?" I shoved up and went to the bar. Opening a cabinet, I retrieved a bottle of scotch and two tumblers. "Matthew, I'm sorry about tonight. I… well I just wanted to show you that I could do the job."

Shaking my head, I purposefully sat on the chair across from her and took a swig. As her pink tongue darted over her lips and she ran a fingertip over the rim of the glass. Time to tell her I'm married.

Chapter 5

Sarah

"Do you like it?" he asks. I suppress my smile. He's beaming, his eyes hopeful, as he waits for me to answer. I look around the big colonial hotel he's just shown me. He's so excited about it—it's a property he built —and I know it makes him feel proud. He's imagining all the possibilities, and he sees himself here penthouse.

"What do you think?" he says, almost bursting at the seams.

"I love it," I finally reveal with a large smile. He picks me up, kisses me, and spins me around. He sees himself here, and I see myself wherever he is. "This is where our life starts," he says, holding me close.We definitely need a fresh start. The last year had been a complete hell.

"I was hoping you'd say that," he says triumphantly. "There's one more thing I have to show you."

I look at him quizzically, but I love surprises. He takes my hand and leads me outside to the balcony I saw when we first came into the room. He stands in front of the door and tells me to close my eyes.

I giggle. I hear the door open then feel his hands cover my eyes as he ushers me into it.

"Your eyes are still closed?" I nod. I feel his hands leave my eyes. "Look up," he says. When I do, my jaw drops.

I'm staring up at the massive billboard opposite the penthouse with my picture on it and the words 'New York Times best seller - Sarah Davidson '.

"Oh my, what…how?" I stammer.

"Your publisher called today while you were out and told me."

I turned to face Matthew. "Oh, Matthew this is so wonderful, I don't deserve this." Tears streamed down my face. "This year, its just been…"

"Shh, sweetheart I know. You deserve this,

you're the most wonderful reason I ever met."
Matthew held me close. "Let me get us a drink."

Chapter 6

Matthew

I held our drinks. I watched her carefully, searching for signs of the emotion she found she'd run out of. She didn't have tears left for any of them. Not right now. She had reached her threshold.

"Yeah, sometimes I think I'm not such a good person to know," she said and shook her head. "I've done things you wouldn't believe, Matthew," she told me. "I'm not who you thought I was. I'm not who I thought I was."

Things had been better between them after Eden had shot me and then later died in my office.

It had been a mess. Sarah had been so naïve then — so naïve compared to what she was now. She closed her eyes and inhaled deeply through her nostrils, exhaled. When she opened them again I was next to her. She accepted her tumbler and they drank together.

She leaned towards me. "I want a kiss.'

My face screwed up, and for an instant my stubborn composure cleared away to reveal a deep hurt. "I want more than a kiss, Sarah,' he said. He slowly placed my glass on the bed cover and she leaned in to me and pressed her lips to mine. A rush of pleasure and emotion came to the surface as they kissed. Mouth to mouth. Tongue to tongue. It felt fucking good to kiss him again. She dropped her empty glass and it rolled off the edge of the bed, hitting my foot and landing on the hotel carpet.

"Fuck!"

Sarah laughed.

I turned and pushed her down on the bed, propping myself up on my arms above her.

"Think that's funny, hey?" I gently touched her face and ran my fingers back from her temples and through her blonde hair while she looked up at me, liking what she saw. Instinctively, her body rose to meet mine, one long leg twining around me. I lowered my face to her, my light stubble brushing her cheek. They locked together. Their problems, their history, all the things that had come between them seemed not to matter in that moment. All that mattered was that they were together, finally, right here, right now. She pulled at my buttons, opening my shirt and running her hands over my warm skin, the soft hairs of my chest. I sat up and pulled my shirt off and she did the same. I ran my eager fingers over her black bra and pushed my face into her cleavage, inhaling her. She unclipped her bra, freeing her breasts, then pulled the rest of her clothes off, tossing her jeans and underwear on the hotel-room floor. My intense blue eyes took her in hungrily. When I pushed her legs open and went down on her, I looked up for a moment. They locked eyes.

"I love you, Sarah."

My tongue darted out and she closed her eyes, arching her back.

Sarah held her orgasm for what seemed an eternity. When it finally crashed, the pleasure rippled out like waves through her whole body, shooting up through her arms and out through her fingertips. She shuddered and sighed beneath me as I raised myself up between her legs and undid the buttons on my jeans. She felt my bare cock push at the hollow between her legs and she lifted herself and ground her hips against me, teasing. She was wet and warm, and once she could wait no longer she grabbed my arse and asked for what she wanted, whispering in my ear. I slid inside her inch by inch, gasping with every millimetre of progress.

"Yes …" she whispered with her mouth, as if her body was not already saying it louder.

They rolled to one side across the stiff hotel sheets and she pulled herself atop me, barely keeping me inside her for a moment. I held her hips as she leaned over me and inhaled the nape of my strong neck, her plump lips pressed to my stubble, smelling that masculine scent she'd always found so intoxicating — a scent like honeyed spice. Slowly, she slid her hand across my firm chest, from one nipple to the other, and pushed her hips down. I arched beneath her, body tense, impatient. She rose again until both of my hands grasped her buttocks, begging her not to move. She slowly slid back over my length, and I tilted my head back.

"Fuck."

Again and again she slid over me.

I gripped her.

It was over too fast. So they began again and took their time.

Chapter 7

Jeanette

I sat sipping my coffee. Not that fancy crap that Matthew made me get for Sarah nope. I'm a straight up black coffee, the stronger the better. I needed it after the morning I'd had. 'New York Times best seller - Sarah Davidson '. I'd seen the sign as I drove through the city before Matthew had even had a chance to gloat about it at the office. Sarah is really pissing me off now. She needed to be dealt with once and for all. But how? How can I get rid of Sarah.

My fingers tapped against the paper cup. What's better to break up a marriage then infidelity. If I can't make Matthew want me then I will just have to make it so Sarah doesn't want him.

Heartbroken Matthew, will just need some extra special comforting after that. Especially now that I know I'm three months pregnant with Eden's baby. My baby will need his daddy.

*****

My stomach feels as if it's on a roller coaster as I stand in the foyer of his penthouse apartment after I've rung the bell twice. I hear his footsteps approaching. When he opens the door, I swallow my nerves. His eyes widen, and a bright smile spreads across his face.

"Jeanette, it's good to see you," he says. I feel relieved that he's excited to see me after I practically ran away from him like a crazy person the last time I saw him.

"I'm glad you said that. I just wanted to apologize for how I acted at the restaurant," I say, folding my hands together. He gives me a sexy smirk—I wonder if he knows it's sexy.

"No, you were fine. I just—I was a little confused." He chuckles while leaning in the doorway.

"I can see how you would be," I say with a

giggle, sweeping my hair over my shoulder. I rub my arms to signal I'm cold.

"Can I come in?"

His eyes meet mine, and I see him swallow hard. Does he know?

"Sure," he says after a moment of hesitation. I smile gratefully. He steps back and allows me to pass. It's been a long time since I've come into the penthouse, I hadn't been here since Matthew had been shot by Eden.

The TV is blasting one of those sports stations Matthew watch. He has a pizza box open on the table and a bottle of scotch sitting next to it.

He walks past me and turns down the television. He looks a little embarrassed, and it's cute. He runs his hands through his hair. We stand around awkwardly for a minute. In my wildest dreams, I'd just walk up and kiss him, but I didn't factor in that he's so much taller than me. He'd have to let me pull his head down or lift me up to kiss him, and I'm not strong enough to force him without this going extremely wrong. Fuck, I should have worn taller heels, but that would have been stupidly obvious.

"Can I sit?" I ask, feeing all the butterflies that

lie dormant when I'm around any other boy wake up and parade around my stomach.

"Sure," he says, gesturing to the couch. I sit and try to inconspicuously let out a deep breath. He sits in the chair across from me and leans forward, his elbows resting on his knees. He's so relaxed, more than I've ever seen him before.

"So that day at the restaurant when you ran out," he asks, but not in a way that makes me feel awkward. He's not stiff and distanced as he was that day. He seems… curious maybe. I smile.

"I shouldn't have run out like idiot." He smiles one of his glorious smiles that makes my heart flutter.

"I was embarrassed," I say, feeling my nerves getting the best of me. He nods with a glimmer of a grin. He clasps his big hands, and my eyes drift to the tattoo on his arm. I want to touch it. I want to rest on it. I want to live there on his moon hidden away behind the clouds.

"I figured that," he says, his voice like a lullaby.

"I never meant to make you feel that way." He sighs, and I can see clouds form behind his bright eyes.

"I don't know if I did something to make you

feel too..." His eyes are glued to his hands. He's moving around in his seat... No, no, no. This conversation is about to go in a direction I definitely don't want it to go.

"You didn't do anything," I say. I'm afraid he'll say something that will destroy the courage I've mustered to come here, killing any spunk I have now.

"It's not what you do." His eyes reluctantly meet mine. Colour rises in his cheeks.

"It's just who you are. It's how you make me feel—your voice, your energy. Everything about you made me say what I said that day," I say, begging his eyes to meet mine. They do but only briefly. He sits back in the chair and lets out a deep sigh, picks up a tumbler near the scotch bottle, and takes a swig from it. He shakes his head.

"You don't know what you're saying, Jeanette."

"That's not it!" I shake my head.

"Jeanette, I-I'm flattered, believe me," he says, his blue eyes on mine, and I feel my heart sink.

"But I can't—you can't, you can't say things like that to me." His voice is soft, caring, and it warms up every part of me regardless of his words.

"I meant every word! No one makes me feel

how I do when I'm around you."

At this point, I'm desperate. I have one shot, and since I'm going to walk away from this embarrassed no matter what, I want to leave with no regrets. He looks at his feet.

His head snaps up. "It is. I promise you, Jeanette. You need to leave before you do something you'll really regret," he says as if it pains him. I stand and take a deep breath. My heart feels as if I'm running a marathon.

I walk to him and stand between his legs. He looks up at me confused, almost afraid, but there's something else I can't read. Whatever that is, even if it's just curiosity, it drives me onward.

"Do you not feel anything?" I ask, my voice barely above a whisper. I'm standing over him, and he leans back, looking at me. I've never been this close to him. My legs are against his knees, and even though he's not touching me per se, my entire body is on edge and warm. I can't leave this house without kissing those perfect lips that seem to be quivering right now.

"Jeanette, please." His voice has dropped an octave, and I feel as if it's vibrating through me. His eyes drift over my body, taking in every inch of me, and my stomach clenches. Just the way he's looking at me has made me hotter than anything any boy has ever done to me. He swallows hard. I see the conflict in his expression. He's fighting a silent battle with himself, and I want him to lose.

"You're a very beautiful woman, but what you're saying—doing—is crazy—"

That's the last word he says before I silence him with my lips. The second I do, it's as if my body wakes up. I feel every nerve in it. His lips are so soft, and they're still but parted just enough for me to take his upper lip in my mouth. I gently bring my hands to the back of his head and run my hands through his hair.

Our lips fit perfectly together, and even though he's perfectly still, it beats every other kiss I've ever experienced. I feel the anticipation building. He hasn't pushed me away, and that's all the invitation I need for more. I climb on his lap, wrap my arms around his neck, and feel fire move through my body as I kiss him a little more tenderly. When his hands move to my waist and he pulls me closer, I feel faint. His mouth opens, and his tongue enters my mouth, filling it. His kiss is artful and more experienced than any other I've had.

I feel heavy but light-headed as our kiss gets deeper, so deep I feel as if I'll be one with him soon. The longer I kiss him, our tongues devouring one another's, the more heat comes between my legs. It's frustrating but the best feeling I've ever had. I feel his length press against me, this what should have been mine all along, I lean in and feel it pressed between my thighs. I let out a soft moan while our tongues wrap around each other's.

I press against it again and faster and faster. I can't control the whimpers coming out of my mouth.

He starts to guide my hips against him, aiding me in the absolute pleasure building and building. His own breathing becomes deeper. It's coming faster and faster. I'm no longer kissing him. My head is thrown back as I concentrate on feeling him through the hard, rough jeans that feel like heaven through my cotton underwear, which is soaked. He squeezes my butt and presses me hard against him, and his mouth starts to devour my neck, sucking in my skin like it's air he needs to breath.

We move in sync, rhythmically, more rapidly, desperately. I dig my fingers into the couch, clawing it as I move against him. Then, I feel an explosion that no boy has ever been able to make me feel, and as I tumble over the edge, I moan his name loudly, and I can't stop panting. My legs are quivering, and the hardness I felt underneath me is gone. We sit there, both catching our breath, my body still reeling. I rest my head in the crook of his neck and feel our hearts beating in sync. I lean back to look at his face. His gaze is on the ceiling. Tiny sweat beads are on his forehead, and I wipe them. His eyes are closed, and his breathing normalizes. When it does, his eyes almost snap open, and he looks at me. For the first time, his eyes don't smile at me. They're like glass. I think there are tears in them, and that scares me.

I climb off him. He stands and glares at me, not with anger just confusion. He walks quickly out of the room, and I hear him cursing. I can't exactly understand what he's said, but I know he's upset. I sit there, unsure of what to do. Should I say something to him? I can't think of anything that will comfort him. Matthew he be mad if I'm still here when he comes back?

What I feel is real, and what we just did, what I just experienced with him, I won't be able to just forget. I don't want to forget it. I want to relive it over and over. I want what we had back. He was mine first.

"Jeanette?" he calls. I think he's in their bathroom. I take a deep breath.

"Yes?"

"Can you please leave?"

My heart drops, and I feel tears in my eyes.

"Uh, sure."

My voice sounds weak and broken. I slowly get off the couch and look back to where he is in the penthouse. I can't see him, but I know he's there. A part of me wants to go to him and make him look at me, another part of me says I don't deserve to make demands, and the other part of me just wants to slink away. Once my legs regain their balance, walk around to the sink and open the slide out bin below . If he won't take me then I will just have to force things along. I dropped the opened pack from my purse and making sure it would be well visible when Sarah returns.

Chapter 8

Sarah

I couldn't believe what I had just seen. Jeanette. She hadn't seen me as I walked across the other side of the building lobby. It was ten o'clock at night. I had been at a book signing in Geelong to come back to this. Why had she been here so late? And dressed like that? No.. Surely not. Matthew would never. I enter the pin to the key pad and stride through the apartment.

"Matthew"

"I'm in here. " he wonders out from the bathroom. "Hey, sweetheart, how was your book signing?" He says leaning forward to kiss me reeking of scotch.

Placing both hands on his chest I push him away.

"Why was Jeanette here? I saw her in the lobby."

I start picking up the empty glass and pizza box left on the counter.

"She was just dropping off some paperwork I need for my meeting first thing tomorrow" his reply nonchalant.

I open the bin below the sink to place the remains of pizza in. I still. A pregnancy test box.

No.

No.

No.

This can't be happening.

I lift up the box staring at it. A piece of paper shoved down beside the stick that clearly says pregnant.

Congratulation on becoming a dad Matthew.

I will love you always.

J x

* * *

He lied to me. What's worse than him lying to me as my husband, my so-called soul mate, is that he lied to me as my friend. Our history, our bond, our love, didn't stop my best friend from lying to me all these years. He kept secrets from me, and it hurts. It hurts so badly—the half-truths, the deception, the words I never ever thought I'd use… it all hurts.

I never thought that anything associated with love could be so painful, but love betrayed definitely is. This unfathomable heartache snuffs out all of my urges toward forgiveness because now I know the truth. At least what I imagine the truth to be—those images run continuously through my mind.

The love that once was so sure has been replaced by anguish . A pain that erases the joy and closeness we shared, pushing it further and further away, like a mirage—unreal. Our history seems more like an illusion. Only vague images of our love and life together remain, but those spectral images are tainted.

While my own memories are like a half-forgotten dream, those moments I imagine are all too vivid. Everywhere I look, I see betrayal, and I can't get his duplicitousness out of my head. My faith has been shaken to the core. Those thoughts become an unbearable weight, a sickening fog that suffocates me, a stench so bad it chokes all the beauty and joy out of life. All that remains is blinding rage, anger, bitterness, and hatred. These thoughts turn my consciousness into an abyss that I can't escape. I secretly pray for the moment I'll feel nothing because anything is better than this.

Adultery.

Affair.

Betrayal.

Words I try to escape from as the hours tick by. It feels like time has slowed down, but in reality it is moving so fast it sneaks up on me—like a thief in the night. I look in the mirror at the fine lines that have formed around my mouth and eyes, things I overlooked before but are like flashing lights now. I wonder when this happened? Did it happen with Eden, or did it happen when Matthew was shot? Is today just the first day I noticed them? This morning when I looked in the mirror, I didn't see them, but they were there. Right? I just never noticed until now. I wasn't even alarmed by the increasing number of grey hairs I've accumulated over the years. Why should I worry over trivial things like that anyway when there's so much more to regret?

I always knew life was precious. You realize it when you find out you'll never be able to produce it. When you find out that you're unable to do the one thing you believe you were put on the planet to do— your God-given right as a woman to bear children. I have come to appreciate that fertility is a gift, not a right, even though I'm slightly resentful.

The realisation of just how precious the gift of life is became even more evident once I heard the words, "You have cancer." Ageing, living is a blessing, not something to worry about. When I was able to say, "I beat cancer," I quit worrying about the small things. If I could survive cancer, I could survive anything. To wake up in the morning and take a breath became so much more of a welcome event than one would ever think.

So it isn't a wonder why today, of all days, I notice the things I didn't use to care about but today mean everything. I wish I were just being dramatic, but without hesitation, I can say being alive doesn't seem as important as it once was.

These badges of maturity feel less like an honor and more like a punishment, a cruel inside joke I'm not in on.

What else could I think of it as? My husband, my dear husband, the man I love more than anything in the entire world, has always made me feel beautiful. When I said wrinkles, he said laugh lines, and not only that, he said they made me more beautiful than the day he first met me. I believed him.

I believed him because he's my best friend, my confidant, my own personal superhero... or at least he was yesterday. Today, he's my personally-crafted villain.

One who knows my weaknesses and knows me better than anyone else in the world. I've shared my deepest secrets with him. He's been my glue when my world was on the cusp of falling apart several times over— at least I thought he was. Maybe he wasn't, or maybe he was for a while, or maybe it was all a façade.

Maybe I was just a fool. I must have been a fool, an arrogant one. Because until today, I never understood why the women I grew up with felt self-conscious about their appearances as each birthday passed. Because I knew it all, I had it all figured out—they'd married the wrong man. I thought that if you married your soul's true mate, a life partner, they should appreciate who you are now, who you've grown to become. My husband, my best friend, told me that, and like a fool in love, I never once questioned it—until today.

Because today is the day I found out that my husband—my best friend, the man I turned my world upside down for, whom I gave my youth to, my best days, my joy, my entire self—has not only been screwing Jeanette but he'd gotten her pregnant. Before today, I considered her— the thirty-two-year-old without a single laugh line who had been there when no body else had been — like a best friend . But now I know her as my husband's lover.

So today, I look in this mirror and see every single thing that makes me different from the girl he fell in love with and the girl he betrayed me with. Today, I question all the times I stood in front of this mirror, pulling myself together to greet each day with a smile while I fought the flesh-eating monster living inside me, to make life easier for him. Today it all seems pointless, worthless! If I'd just given in when death came for me, I wouldn't be experiencing the pain I'm in now, a fate that seems worse than death. I hate thinking like this! I hate these thoughts, but they're honest and feel more real than anything else today. Truer than love, more honest than forgiveness, and more authentic than the last twenty-five years of what I thought was an unbreakable marriage.

I want to cry and vomit at the same time. Maybe I could just crawl into myself as if I didn't exist. Here I stand, thirty-six years old, a woman and mother who beat the odds of advanced cancer. Yesterday morning, I felt invincible. Now I feel as fragile as a seventeen-year-old whose heart has been broken, crushed, demolished.

A grown woman decimated and paralysed. It's hard to remember how to move. Not so much in the literal sense, even though my limbs feel heavy, but how do I get out of this space I'm in? How do I escape from what feels like a prison? My husband has cheated and broken my trust.

*****

I try to push her name out of my mind because

whenever I think of it, I feel rage boil up from the pit of my stomach. I'm angry at her, at him, at myself. How could I not see it? How could I not have a clue that something was going on between them? How could I not notice my husband was having an affair right under my nose? I have to be the biggest idiot on the planet. Before I step over the kitchen threshold, the smell hits me. As I step in, I see a plate already fixed with waffles, grits, fresh fruit, and sausage.

"Good morning."

I look up and see Matthew step into the kitchen from the pantry. He looks a mess. He looks how I feel. I try to speak, but no words come out of my mouth.

"I-I made breakfast. I tried to make it healthy. You've been talking a lot about that lately, and I've listened," he says, his blue eyes encapsulated by puffy eyelids. His hair is completely disheveled, as if he's run his hands through it a thousand times. His five o'clock shadow is pronounced and his dimples absent because his lips are pressed so firmly together. This is the first time I've looked at him since I found out.

The first time I've ever looked at the man I

married and felt anything but love, hope, and strength. It's funny how a few hours have changed everything for us. Seeing him makes my emotions crash against each other. Each second I stand here, I become more enraged.

How could he do something so stupid, so selfish, and so... unforgivable? And he stands here like nothing has happened, as if we're going to eat breakfast together and everything will be okay?! Nothing will be okay. I realize this as I stand in my kitchen in front of him, the same place he and his whore ate with me and sat with our family and friends.

"I can't believe you did this to us." The words are automatic, as if triggered by his presence. They hurt to speak but hurt even more to hold in.

"Sarah." His voice breaks as he tries to approach me, but I step back and push my arms out to let him know to stay back.

"Please, just let me explain," he begs.

His voice sounds pained, and my heart aches for him—for me "I can't. I can't. I don't want to hear it, and there's nothing that you can explain. Anything you say will only make things worse!"

I'm frantic. It's a lie; I want to know everything,

but I don't think I can survive hearing it.

"Sarah, you're my best friend," he says with tears in his eyes.

I have to turn away. I grab a chair to keep my balance. To see him like this hurts, but I can't hurt for him. He didn't hurt for me. I don't even know if he hurts for me now. I'm sure he hurts for himself.

"I never meant to hurt you. I know how that sounds, but if I could take it back—"

"You did hurt me! Worse than anything I've ever experienced, and you cannot take it back." My voice is loud and unrecognisable. His gaze isn't on me but set on the floor instead.

"In our home, Matthew. How could you? With Jeanette of all people!" I'm close to screaming at the top of my lungs.

"There's no excuse for what I did," he whispers. His words make me want to throw something. To see him broken… I haven't seen him like this since I was sick. A chill shoots down my spine.

"Were you seeing her when I was sick?" I ask cautiously. I don't know if I can take hearing the answer. His eyes widen, and he approaches me; I retreat again.

"No. I stopped before I found out you lost our

child," he promises. The pain of that memory shoots through me. I know he thinks what he said should give me some consolation, but it doesn't. It tears open a wound I've tried to forget, a wound that has become purulent.

"You stopped out of pity. You stopped out of a sense of duty, guilt, and a mournful promise but not out of love. Do you love her?"

He shakes his head. "It's always been you, Sarah—" My eyes narrow on his.

"Except when you were screwing her." He looks defeated, as though he's given up and realised there's absolutely nothing he can say to fix this. I feel as though my soul is beginning to crumble. I can't talk to him about this. I can't think about this.

"I need you to leave."

"Sarah, please. I'll give you time. I owe you that, but we can get past this." His voice deepens with each word to the more familiar, authoritative tone I'm used to from him instead of the sad, broken one.

"How dare you!" I scream. "You cheated on me, Matthew! You got her pregnant ! How can we get past that? Tell me?!" He covers his face.

"I didn't know."

He attempts to touch me again, and I swat him away.

"You didn't know? You think that makes it better?" My whole body shakes as I shed angry tears. Tears are falling down his face now too. He gets on his knees and grabs my waist.

"What can I do? Tell me—what can I do? I'll do anything. Please!"

I try to get out of his grasp, but he holds me tighter.

"We can get through this. I promise you we can."

Chapter 9

Matthew

I can't be here anymore. My heart hurts too much.
Sarah

The penthouse is empty. Sarah is gone, escaped to my stepsister Kelsey's house. She's got a book tour coming up and Sarah's staying in Sydney to finish up her latest book, I think. I hear a lot these days, but it's all jumbled together. It's better that way. I try not to think because thinking reminds me of what I've done, what I've let happen to me.

I've become that guy, that terrible stereotypical man who's cheated on his wife, who's betrayed his family with a younger woman, and I hate myself for it. I hate myself because I was weak and let it happen. I hate myself because there is no tangible reason as to why I've been unhappy. I hate myself because being with her made me happy, made me feel alive again. She brought me back to my old self, but my old self would have never done anything like this. My old self loved Sarah with every part of him every second of the day.

My old self would have died before hurting Sarah. My old self promised he'd protect her from the pain he caused her so many years ago, that she'd never have to experience it again.

The smartest thing I've done in the past year was walk away from Jeanette that night, and I didn't do it until after she'd given me her body willingly, unselfishly, and made it mine. I took her each time knowing that I took a piece of her with me when I left. I saw it in her eyes even when she tried to hide it. I hid from myself that each time I left, I left a part of myself with her.

She looked at me with her big, wide eyes full of

tears and told me she loved me, and I couldn't say it back. I felt terrible—I wanted to be able to say it back more than anything. She wouldn't have understood that would have made things worse. If I'd said those words, it would have made everything worse, intensified things that much more. I care about her, I crave her, I want her, but love… I can't love her the way she needs me to.

You can't love two people at the same time, and even in the state I'm in, my heart belongs to Sarah. It's ridiculous, I know, because I shouldn't be able to cheat if I love Sarah. I've grown selfish. This year has made what I want come first—my priorities have shifted.

It's been two weeks since I woke up in Jeanette's bed. Like an addict, my withdrawal turns me into an asshole. I just have to detox, forget about her, learn to handle things the way I should have in the first place, not like a fifteen-year-old boy with a boner. I have to get back to who I was, fall in love with my wife again. Maybe we should go on a trip. We all need a vacation, especially before her book tour starts. I have to let Jeanette go. She deserves more. I don't want to ruin her.

I head to the kitchen and grab a beer, then

decide to get the scotch I have hidden under the sink instead. The one good thing is I haven't used alcohol as a crutch. The last thing I need is to be a guilty asshole alcoholic. But today I'll give myself a pass since I'm here alone and won't have to look at the hopeless stare Sarah has given for me the past few days.

*****

When the doorbell rings, I'm a little dizzy, the bottle of scotch half empty from when I started. I might have overdone it… I make my way to the door, and when I open it, she's there.

The light at the penthouse illuminates her face, calling attention to her bright, seductive eyes, her plump lips.

She's like a tempting angel. She's breaking the rules.

Rules that she made up the first night after we crossed the line and she said we should have rules to keep things from getting messy, from going bad. One of the rules was for her to never show up here for me, that we'd never be in my house alone. Maybe she doesn't know I'm here alone. But she has to know Sarah isn't here.

"Can I come in?" she asks. It's cold out, freezing. Her cheeks are red. She doesn't have a hat or scarf on, just a coat that really should be classified as a jacket but has fur around the hood.

A little voice in my head says, "Walk her to her car. Tell her you're sorry you ruined her life and she'll find someone who makes her feel the way she says she does with you and who can love her how she wants, how she deserves."

But the other parts of me win out aided by the scotch. I step aside and watch her pass. We stand in the kitchen.

"Is it just us?" she whispers. I nod, and her lips turn upward but not into an actual smile. She begins to take off her coat, and I clear my throat. I see a flicker of anger in her eyes, but she doesn't stop. I stop my eyes from roving her body, reminding myself I know what's under her clothes.

"So you're just done with me now?" she asks quietly.

"Don't make it sound like that," I say in the same volume she uses.

"But that is what you want?" She looks at me with innocent eyes, her expression hurt.

"This isn't good for either of us. Tell me you're happy. You're not happy!" I say in a hushed whisper, my tone sharp. I hope she gets my point.

"You make me happy," she says, looking me in the eye.

"You were happy the last time I saw you?" I ask her sarcastically. She squints at me.

"You're drunk?" I sigh.

"I'm not drunk. I just had a few drinks."

But I think that's a lie because I'm fighting the urge to kiss her, to feel her, to do things I'd never think about doing in this house. It's off-limits, and I was supposed to be ending this. She runs her hand through her hair, gives me a seductive smile, and walks toward me. I swallow hard and step back until I bump into the refrigerator.

"I'm sorry," she says, running her hands up my chest.

"Jeanette, not here." But my words are weak, and my body is even weaker. She looks up at me, and I feel my resolve deteriorating.

"I know you want me," she purrs. Her hands slide down and go inside my pants.

"I can feel how much."

She kisses me, and she does it with everything

in her, all her passion, all her love, all her fear. She emotes, giving herself to me in each kiss, in each touch. She loves purely and selflessly, and she makes me feel how I used to with just a kiss. I get lost in her.

Chapter 10

Sarah

It had been two weeks since I had been home but I couldn't run away to my sisters forever. I had to face reality and at least talk to Matthew about what we were going to do about our marriage.

The Uber slowed in front of our building, and she slipped off her shoes. I could hardly wait to take a shower. I wished I could extricate thoughts of Matthew from her heart as easily as rinsing the scent of him from her skin. As the car stopped, I opened the door, ignoring the driver who rushed to get there first. I waved him off, but gave him a small thank you before running to her building. I punched in the code, and entered. On the way up in the elevator, fresh tears surfaced. My lips pursed in anger.

I couldn't believe that I was even trying to understand what had just happened in any other way than how I'd seen it with her own eyes. A ding alerted her that I'd finally arrived on her floor. The doors opened and I strode Tapping at the security pad, I entered the code. The handle clicked open and I blew out a breath.

"What the hell?" Adrenaline shot through my body as I took in the sight of the overturned sofa. Black dirt splattered across the floor, plants had rolled onto their sides. My desk had been ransacked, my laptop smashed onto the stone tiles.

With my first instinct to call the police, I remembered I'd accidentally left my phone charging in the kitchen. I gasped as I took in the sight of the mess. The cabinets had all been opened, vitamin and prescription bottles scattered across the floor. My heart sank when I looked at her charger, the phone missing from its docking station. I carefully navigated around the shards of broken ceramic plates and spied the edge of her cell peeking out from under the refrigerator. Carefully, I bent to grab it, her fingernails tapping at the edges. An inch further, I thought. When it was within her reach, I retrieved it.

"Please work, please work," I repeated, praying it would recognise her fingerprint. As the biometric lock released and the phone flared to life I exhaled in relief.

"Thank God." Although the web of cracked glass made it difficult to see, I managed to type in 000. My hands shook as it rang. The operator clicked onto the line, and I heard the sound of footsteps. The phone fell from her hands as the blow came to her head. As blackness claimed me, I called Matthew's name.

*****

The woman was leaning over me, her breath putrid and hot against my neck. I tried to spit at her, but the rubber gag caused the spittle to drip from the corners of her mouth, down my chin. She pulled at her restraints, but only felt the twine bite unforgivingly into her flesh. I could see the woman's face clearly so close to hers.

Jeanette.

The lamp light played across a deep gash on her

forehead. The split was long, still oozing blood, but her eyes were alert, alive, dancing in sadistic satisfaction.

"You're drooling, Sarah." Her name sounded loathsome on her lips. He was holding something in her latex-gloved hand…bringing it to her throat. It was a surgical sponge, dripping with disinfectant. He was cleaning her down, removing the river's soil and smell. Her hands slipped over my naked body, over the goose bumps, pausing on my raised nipples. The cloth moved over my breasts, my navel, down my stomach. I tried to close my legs, but my ankles were held too far apart.

I tried to pretend I was somewhere else.

I'm walking on the beach, walking free, not here. Not with that stinging cloth pushed between my legs. Please…

Jeanette turned from me. She was reaching for something, pulling something from her toolbox with both hands. I strained her head, saw a sharp tip. She moved down my body, towards my bound ankles, caressed my bare feet with her fingertips, and slid something around my foot. My shoes! She had fetched her stilettos from the van and was now placing them on her feet.

"Mine…" she sighed.

I felt so groggy. My breath was shallow and laboured and I was trembling. She was walking back to the toolbox, arranging implements, laying them on the plastic sheet, then wiping them clean. I made out what looked like a scalpel, a knife with a long sharp blade, pliers…

I forced her legs back and forth violently. Break the twine! It bit angrily into her. The pain was overwhelming, but I had to keep on. The bed posts protested with loud creaks and strains.

Jeanette stood over me, lips twitching. Her slim, gloved hands held the disinfected scalpel elegantly and her eyes followed the progress of the sharp tip towards my naked body, towards my naked breast, my cold raised nipple. The scalpel blade pressed on my breast, ready to pierce. I wanted to scream. I wanted to fight back. I prayed it would end soon.

Her eyes were so close to mine and yet they were so distant, part of another world I could not comprehend.

"Are you ready, Whore?"

Whore?

Those words, so terrible, spitting from those

mean lips. Are you ready…whore?

"Matthew is mine, he was always mine. You took Eden from me and now whore it's time for you to suffer for all these years you kept him away from me."

I would die now…I was ready to die. Wait. I pulled myself back. That was it! I would pretend. It could stall her. Anything. Try anything.

I rolled my eyes back in my head and shook violently on the bed, convulsing and groaning. The scalpel pricked her as I moved, tearing my skin, but then moved away. I choked on the gag, as convincingly as I could manage. The movement hurt, my ribs screaming out, everything immersed in pain, but the scalpel had pulled away.

She was speaking to me now. What was she saying?

"You forget how patience I am. You're not dying until I say so."

I tried to speak, to demand she release me, but the sounds coming from my throat were inhuman, my jaw too swollen.

"I told you there was to be no talking. And yet you refuse to desist." She shook her head slowly, then smiled and bent over me, placing her hands around my skull. I felt the straps around my head tighten painfully for an instant and then release. She pulled the rubber ball from my broken jaw, strings of blood and saliva hanging from my mouth. I tried to speak. She cocked her head to listen. She was playing with me now, teasing me.

She answered my chokes and moans. "No, I won't let you go. No. But you have such beautiful toes. Lovely toes. Would you like to taste them? Suck them for me?"

I nodded, gurgling a bit as I tried to speak. I looked down to the twine biting through my ankles.

"Remove the twine? No, no. I don't think you're that flexible. No, I'll bring the toes to you. Shove them in your mouth. You can bite down on those pretty polished toenails."

The scalpel moved down my naked skin, down my legs, down to my right foot. She muttered something, "The right foot, because it's right…" She slipped the shoe off and dropped it on the wooden floor.

I closed my eyes, felt the scalpel sink in, the pain hot and unbearable as it sliced through. I screamed, the sound blending with everything.

Noises everywhere, sounds filling my ears, colour danced before my eyes, red, green, swirling, such pain, I was falling away…

A loud blast. She'd shot me, she'd stopped cutting and she'd shot me. She opened my eyes, tears flowing down my face, everything blurry. Something wasn't right, she was still alive. Another blast. Wait—something on me—heavy. Someone… her. The woman. He was on top of me. Red in the air, floating—now falling. Blood? Blood everywhere.

Her face was close to mine, tongue protruding, those shocked eyes staring at me. Her jerking body crushed against mine…a heavy sack of twitching blood and flesh lying across mine.

Words…words in my ears. "It's all over now, Sarah." My name sweet again, no venom in the sound. "You'll be fine. I'm here Sarah, I'm here. Quiet. It's all right. Don't try to speak. You're safe now."

Matthew. The voice was Matthew.

A weight being lifted off me, that convulsing mass taken away. The staring eyes no longer watching. I felt light. my ankles suddenly free, the twine cut away. my wrists now.

Softly—softly, something falling on me, cloth, a blanket covering me. I turned on her side and swept the cloth into me, tears filling my eyes, sobbing with joy and relief, pulling my arms and legs into her, holding myself, holding my pain.

Curled up in a tight ball, they carried me to the ambulance.

Chapter 11

Sarah

I woke to the sound of a single piercing scream.
I could smell smoke and burning flesh — the
sickening mix of cooking skin and hair, like
sulphur and seared meat. I sat up violently and
looked around blinking, my body a tangle of
adrenaline and fear. For a moment I was unsure
whether the scream had been my own.

Yes. You were screaming. Again.

Though I had been sure of the smoke, the air
was clean, my lungs clear. There was no fire. I was
in bed, the early light coming in past the shutters
over the balcony. It was another nightmare. My

subconscious was still in that dank cellar in the Dandenong countryside.

My face was slick with sweat and my stomach felt dangerously queasy. I stifled a gag, and quickly realised there was more. No, I thought as I pulled the bed covers off and ran through the spinning dark for the nearby toilet, a hand over my mouth.

I had just made it inside the black-tiled cubicle when my stomach emptied itself through my fingers. There wasn't much there, but I managed to aim what there was at the open toilet. With a ferociousness that surprised me, I gagged and choked until the feeling passed, then sat back on my heels, disgusted. I flushed, closed the lid, wiped my mouth. Cold water felt good on my hands, growing warmer as the pipes woke. I washed my hands and kept the tap running so I could splash my face. Dammit. Face wet and eyes half closed, I stepped across the narrow hallway to the bathroom and flicked the light on. A bottle of spring water sat next to the sink and I used it to rinse my mouth and brush my teeth once, twice. Still, the acid taste remained. My eyes strayed to the small bottle of red door on the toiletries shelf. I gave the top two quick squeezes and the air filled with the distinctive, musky floral scent. I brushed my teeth again.

Eden and Jeanette were dead.

I leaned on the rim of the sink with both hands and looked into the mirror, where a curvy, naked woman with bone-straight blonde hair greeted me. The light cast unflattering shadows, accentuating the jut of my collarbone and the contours of body. I'd been exercising using the dumbbells and chin-up bar I'd found in the man's apartment — push-ups, tricep dips, pull-ups — and my thin arms appeared uncharacteristically ropey and tight. My breasts were full and round, but beneath them were the first signs of increasingly taut abdominal muscles and the hint of ribs. The soft taper of my hips had been reduced to angles and hipbones, something I had not seen in my mirror since my teenage years l over a two decades earlier. I'd dropped a dress size, maybe more. I preferred my softer, curvier self, but weight was sliding off my like water. It's stress, I told myself. I'd have to fight to keep weight on, to stay fit. I needed my strength. Displeased, I leaned in, tilted my head down and pressed my clean fingers to the part in my hair. A pale band of dark blonde roots already showed through. In only another week it would be obvious, the part giving the unsettling effect of a bald stripe. I'd need to dye my hair again. I had resisted the urge to give myself a short chop, such was the identifying flag that had been my once blonde mane. But long hair provided some semblance of cover, I had decided; and, after it had been dyed and chemically straightened, I felt it bore no resemblance to my former style. The black hair hung like a curtain, casting new shadows on the angles of my high cheekbones and falling straight and shiny past my freshly muscled shoulders, contrasting with fair, unblemished skin.

Unblemished, except in the places where I had scars.

The thin, raised cicatrices weren't obvious unless you knew where to look. Unless you knew what they meant.

Chapter 12

Matthew

Sarah was waiting for me at the base of another set of stairs. Her cheeks looked rosy, her breath visible in the cold night air. She smiled broadly as she took in the view, hands on hips and standing tall. Matthew resisted the urge to bundle her into my arms and lift her off the ground. She used to love that. She had said that he made her feel as light as a feather.

Oh fuck it. I want to kiss her.

But he didn't. He didn't pick her up, either. I kept my hands firmly in my jeans' pockets and stared in the direction of the ocean. The view from where they stood was breathtaking, but he could hardly focus on it. He had begun to feel regret that they were not truly sharing the moment—Jeanette's unexpected confession before dying ad put an end to the Eden and Jeanette sagas—the way they once would have, the way he had imagined they would when all the drama was over.

The whole experience had brought them together, but eventually pulled them apart. They should have been kissing, laughing, enjoying the victory together. We should be making love, he thought. He could barely think or breathe for all the restraint it took to stop myself embracing her. It didn't feel right to be so impersonal with her like this.

Matthew felt a fingertip on my wrist, and jumped. It was Sarah's hand searching for mine. She had moved closer. He pulled my hand out of my pocket and squeezed hers, unsure whether it was safe to be even that intimate. Her hand felt smooth and cool in mine. For a while they stayed that way, holding hands and looking out to sea.

"My God, Matthew. What happened with us?"she said with a tremor in her voice. "Was it a mistake from the start? All of it?"

I didn't reply. He pulled her in front of me and gazed into her face in the low light. It was lovely to see her up close. The wind blew her hair back, and the distant lights of Bell's beach glowed like a halo around her head. Her eyes looked into mine, speaking silent emotions that he could not read. He wanted to tell her all the things he had felt in the past few months, but could not find the words. It didn't matter. In the dark, Sarah leaned into me until her lips met mine. Her kiss was a shock of cold from the wind, then warm and welcoming inside her mouth. The surprise of it jolted me into arousal. There she was, her fingers touching my arms, her tongue running slowly across my lips. He parted my lips further and kissed her deeper. Harder. He felt her exhale and melt into me. Her fingers slid across the back of my neck, gently pulling me into her. I bent to meet her, allowing myself the pleasure of her kiss, unsure how long it might last. Now she was pressed firmly against me, her body like a puzzle piece filling every gap between them seamlessly, knee to knee, groin to groin, the swell of her breasts crushed against me. My blood surged at the feel of her, and some part of myself let go. He cradled her in my arms as he had always loved to. It felt so damn good. It felt right. He wanted to swallow her up with my rage and pleasure and anger and love. He loved her so damn much and nothing ever seemed to work between them.

Was it worth it to allow themselves this? Was it worth the gamble?

Yes.

I had no choice. I picked Sarah up and carried her. She clung to me, kissing, squeezing, encouraging. I didn't put her back down until they were near the edge of the tall cliffs, metres away, by the entrance to a rocky nook. Nothing but raging seas and whipping wind surrounded them. There was no one to see. With unspoken understanding, they crawled into the small shelter together, not even registering the cold, uncomfortable rock beneath them. Guarded from the elements, they kneeled torso to torso and began a slow ritual of sensual reacquaintance, hands reaching eagerly for every part of one another. I slid my grateful hands under Sarah's coat and the soft fabric of her knitted top. Her skin felt warm and silky to my touch, my fingers seeming far too rough to be permitted such a pleasure. Sarah's mouth felt hot and willing on mine, her writhing form pushing me to a point of carnal urgency. I was painfully hard, my body eager. She squeezed my arse and ground my erection into her. Her fingers found me, caressing the shape of me through the restraints of my clothing.

"Fuck me, Matthew," she whispered. "Please."

I pushed her down without hesitation. She gave welcomingly under my weight, wrapping her long legs tightly around my hips. Eagerly, she pulled at my belt buckle, tugging until I was free and pressed rigid against her thighs.

*****

I woke, my body tightly spooned against Sarah's. I contemplated the past twenty-four hours, wondering how things had escalated out of control. Pushing the envelope of where she'd go sexually had started off as a game of sorts. I sought to teach her the high that came with risking everything. But with each lesson, I was the one who'd been schooled. When she'd done as I'd asked, telling me to lick her pussy, I'd just about exploded right then. I laughed to myself, recalling how she'd bit me.

Like a wild animal, she'd gone feral, losing herself in the moment. She could kill me, but I reasoned I'd love every second.

I inwardly cursed, aware that I'd almost fucked her without a condom. They hadn't talked about getting back together or about their marriage, let alone having unprotected sex. Yet in the shower, all I'd wanted to do was bury myself deep inside her, my bare skin touching hers. If I were truthful, I'd admit that an unfamiliar desire to have her barefoot and pregnant. The thought of it was ridiculous, I knew. As she stirred in my arms, I briefly considered what it would be like to let go.

This morning, all I wanted to do was make love to her again. My lips grazed over Sarah's neck, my tongue brushing onto her skin. She tasted like honey butter, salty and sweet. Her nipple peaked underneath my fingertips and my arousal spiked. My hand glided down to her mound, and without saying a word, she parted her legs, giving me access to her already drenched pussy. I plunged a finger into her core, testing her readiness, and she rocked into my hand.

"Hmm, Matthew," she moaned.

"Give me a minute," I said, reaching for

protection. Using my teeth, I tore it open and slipped it onto my hard length. I rolled Sarah onto her back and her eyes blinked open at me. She gave me a sleepy smile and my heart caught. For the love of all that was holy, he'd never seen a more beautiful sight. Her tousled hair spread all over the pillow, her hands off to the side.

"Good morning, sweetheart," I said, guiding my cock to her entrance. "Good morning." Sarah closed her eyes and moaned as I slowly pressed into her.

"Ah, yes."

"You are so damn sexy." As I rocked into her, fully sheathing myself, I dropped my head to her breast, suckling a taut tip.

"Hmm… delicious."

I gave equal attention to her other nipple, eliciting soft cries. She raked her fingers into my hair, cradling my head to her chest.

"You feel so good inside me," she told me.

"Not nearly as good as you feel around me." I lifted my gaze to meet hers, and my chest filled with emotion. Jesus Christ almighty, I could make love to this woman all day and it would never be enough.

I kissed her, sucking her bottom lip, and softly nipping it. As she moaned and raised her hips to meet mine, I thrust upward, brushing my pelvis against her clit. My fingers wrapped around her wrists, and I pinned her arms to either side of her head. As she exposed her neck to me, my lips moved to her collarbone.

"Matthew, I'm… yes, yes, yes," she mumbled as I took her.

Writhing underneath my muscular torso, she screamed my name. Her pussy pulsated around my cock as she came hard. Plunging into her, I lost control as she fisted my shaft. The waves of my release claimed me, and I pressed my lips to hers, passionately kissing her. Slowly breaking contact, I opened my eyes and caught her wanton gaze. Sarah blinked and gave a small laugh.

"Something funny, Mrs Davidson?"

"I never get these kinds of wake up calls when I'm at my sisters," she teased.

"I certainly hope not."

"I could do this with you every morning," she said. As if she realised what she'd implied, she averted her gaze.

"So could I, sweetheart." Her eyes darted to my

and the reticence lingered before he continued.

"How are you feeling this morning?"

"How do I feel?" She smiled. "I feel great."

"Do you want to sleep a little more?"

"Hmm... maybe."

I knew she needed more rest, and I probably did too, but more than that, I needed space. It was far too soon to think Sarah would come home, but in my heart, it was exactly what I desired.

Chapter 13

Sarah

Every morning Matthew had woken me up the same way for a month. His body in sync with mine doing what we knew best.

"You're mine, Sarah." He moaned helplessly.

"Yes."

"Your body is mine," he said, and thrust two long fingers deep inside me. I inhaled sharply, and my hips instinctively jerked forward.

"Yes."

"Your orgasms are mine."

He glided his thumb across my clitoris, adding just enough pressure and friction to make me tremble with a need only he knew how to appease. My eyes darkened with desire as I rolled my hips, seeking the release he was holding just out of my reach.

"Yes."

He skimmed his lips up to my ear, his breath hot and damp against my skin.

"I own you, Sarah. Heart and soul," he no longer cared how possessive or barbaric he sounded.

"Always," I whispered, my reply heartfelt and true.

"I will fucking kill any man who dares to touch you without my permission." He knew how ruthless his tone sounds, but his threat real.

"You belong to me. Only me. Do you understand?"

I lifted a hand and touched his face, forcing him to look into eyes.

"Yes, I'm yours, Matthew. There's only ever been you."

The End of

Revenge Games

Sinful Games

This page is intentionally left blank

Chapter 1

Sarah

Everything in our lives is perfect well almost. It has been five years since the day that I almost died. Five years and yet the scars still show on my body. My husband Matthew still wakes with night terrors each night and they have only gotten worse since our beautiful daughter Katherine was born. Katherine Paige Davison, born November 25th 2018, eight pounds 11 ounces. The most wonderful moment of my life.

Matthew and I on a babymoon on the Central Coast of New South Wales. Soaking up the sun, drinking mocktails and reading as many of Audrey Carlan's International Guy novels as I possibly could. I was madly in love with SkyPark.

At first I think I've accidentally wet the bed. The baby's been doing gymnastics with my bladder a lot lately, so it's the first thing that comes to mind. Except I'm soaking and the cramps I'm nursing feel way more intense than I'm used to. I sit up and toss the covers aside. My suspicions are immediately confirmed. The baby's early.

"Matthew," I breathe, my heart racing so hard in my chest that it threatens to rattle loose. I grab Matthew by the shoulder and shake him as hard as I can.

"Matthew, the baby's coming."

"Huh, wha—" Matthew mumbles as he wakes.

"What?"

"My water just broke."

Matthew jumps out of bed so fast that he defies the rules of physics, landing with a surprising amount of agility for a man his size. He runs around the foot of the bed to get to me, immediately propping me up with pillows. He's surprisingly calm, all things considered. Though he looks absolutely frazzled what with his hair flat on one side from sleeping and his gray sleep shirt all wrinkled at the edges.

"Everything's going to be okay," he tells me, brushing my hair back with his fingers. His cool hands are a momentary relief against my blazing skin.

"Breathe in through your nose, out through your mouth. Sarah, look at me."

He demonstrates, breathing in and out with me as I grip his hand for support and comfort. I squeeze as hard as I can, trying to focus on the warmth of his palm. If I hurt him, Matthew doesn't let me see. Dialing 000 I hear him rattle of the details to the emergency services.

Hang up the phone and grabbing hold of my hand "You're doing great."

Sweat drenches my forehead. The pain radiating from my core is like nothing I've ever experienced before. I've had my fair share of painful period cramps, but this? I can't even quantify how many times more awful it is. The muscles in my back are tense to the point of snapping. A thousand dull knives stab my gut. Every inch of my body burns as fire fills my blood.

""She's early. Why's she early?" I ask, frantic. The back of my throat is so dry it feels like sandpaper.

"Sarah, I need you to relax. I've got you. It's going to be fine."

Banging on the hotel room door draws my attention from Matthew.

BANG, BANG BANG
"New South Wales Ambulance"
Matthew lets go of my hand rushing to the door. As

the two paramedics enter, pain spikes through me again.

Fuck

"Let's take a look shall we the female paramedic"
nods at me before placing and my knees spreading them
slightly. "Okay folks, looks like we aren't going to be
making it to Gosford hospital after all. She's crowning,"
She tells me steadily. I look at Matthew scared stiff.

"What's your name sweetheart?" the other
paramedic asks.

"Sarah" I grit out as another contraction starts.

"Sarah when I tell you I need to push. Push with the
contractions. Push for ten seconds, and then breathe in
and out. Got it?"

All I could do is nods as my face crumples in, eyes
sealing shut as I shout in agony. Then huff, grits my
teeth together as the next contraction comes.

"Your doing great, now when the next one comes I
need you to push until I say so"

Nodding frantically the next contraction hit.

"Push, push, push, push" the paramedic coaxes. The
next hing I hear is our daughter as she starts crying,
gasping in a huge breath before wailing loudly. The
sound is piercing, abrasive. The most beautiful thing
I've ever heard in my life.

Turning my head to look at Matthew my heart

soared. His grin from ear to ear and absolute
unconditional love in his eyes.

"Sarah, did you hear me?" Matthew's voice pulls me from memories of the past.

"Umm, sorry. What did you say?" I shake my hear clearing my thoughts. How long had he been speaking. Oh, that's right we had been arguing about the fact he seemed to be MIA in our marriage.

"Sarah, I told you, I am only trying to protect us," he sighed

"Bullshit. That's fucking bullshit." I fight the urge to roll my eyes. This isn't getting us anywhere.

"You're hiding Matthew. You are using Katherine as an excuse to avoid the past. To avoid what happened before she were born."

"I am fucking not" he snidest.

"You are, and your just pushing me away. What happened with Eden and Jeanette is five years ago now. They can't hurt us anymore. Only you can, things don't change" I pop myself off the breakfast bar and walk to Matthew placing my hands on his chest. "Matthew, I need you."

"You have me. I'm right here."pulling me closer and placing his chin on my head.

"That's not what I mean, I need who you use to be not this...Ever since Katherine was born you hovering around every minute of everyday. You treat us like we are glass about to break. It's suffocating" I sigh. Matthew's arms drop and he steps away from our embrace.

"Matthew"

"I thought you wanted me here, with you. Clearly I was wrong." Matthew turns and walks towards his office slamming the door closed after he entered. I can't help the tears streaming down my face. It wasn't the first fight we had about the state of our marriage. I fear I'm losing my husband. The husband I use to have that wanted me like I was his next breath.

Chapter 2

Matthew

I thought she needed me but maybe I was wrong. She said that I'm suffocating her. I just can't let any one hurt them. Not ever again. Jeanette had almost taken her from me. If we had of been just one minute later Sarah would be dead. The night still haunts my dreams. Sarah's blood pooling on the floor, her lifeless body. Vomit rises in my throat.

Fuck

I run to my office bathroom, heaving into the toilet.

Turning the faucet off after washing the vomit from my chin, I started at myself in the mirror.

I need to fix this. I need to fix us. But how? Marriage counselling? Divorce… FUCK NO! Take her back to Highclere? Ok, that's not a bad idea.

She was always writing menage in her books. Maybe that's what her fantasy is. Just the thought of Sarah naked kneeling for me before watch her suck another mans cock made me hard instantly.

Fuck.

The more I thought about it the more it made sense. Sarah and I needed more and this way I could give here everything and there was only one man I trusted enough to care for Sarah like I do and that was Connor.

Connor had been my right hand man for almost fifteen years when it came to business. We had done our carpentry apprenticeships together and when I needed things done, Connor made it happen. He and Sarah got along great. Every time we caught up the two would talk for hours and had a banter like long lost friends. We even made him Katherine's god father at her christening. I trust him with my life.

As I picked up my phone and dialled Connor, a strange feeling washed over me. Was I prepared to share my wife? Sure, I had share women before with Eden but the thought had never entered my head when it came to Sarah. I was a complete caveman when it came to her. The phone rang in my ear.

Connor: Hey mate, what's up?

Matthew: I need a favour and you're the only man I trust enough to do this. It's to do with Sarah.

Connor: Mate you know I would do anything for you and Sarah, absolutely anything.

With a sigh of relief, Connors words made up my mind for me. I had to do this. It was the only way to save my marriage. Now I only hope that Sarah will still want me after all this time.

*****

I'd spent the rest of the day in my home office working on a new high-rise proposal. By the time I'm done I walk down the hall to find Kathrine is sound asleep in her bed. My baby girl. My heart melts every time I see her. Leaning down I kiss her forehead and whisper goodnight. Time to find Sarah and try and reclaim what's left of our marriage.

As I enter our master suite I hear the shower running. Sarah doesn't see me as I enter as the room is already filled with steam. Stepping past the glasswork partisan of the double shower I take in everything that is my gorgeous wife. She is fucking stunning. My cock jumps to attention the moment I lay my eyes on her.

The shower was hitting her breasts, gently fondling her nipples, until it rolled down her stomach and onto the tiled floor. Biting back a growl, I place my hand on the wall above her heard blasting my front to her back. A slight jump from Sarah at the surprise that I'd joined her in the shower before she melted back into me. My hard cock perfectly place at the apex of prefect arse.

"Matthew" she moaned as place my other hand over her heated mound. I couldn't let the water distract me from pleasuring her. The water gave him an extra little challenge.

Slinging my fingers between her wet folds and

caused him to breathe deeply through his mouth, while inhaling her scent and exhaling, even more, warmth against her clitoris. My licks got harder and deeper. I was enjoying being this close to her, hearing her sighs, feeling her quiver, causing her legs to tremble.

"God I miss this. You taste fucking amazing. Even sweeter than before."

Pushed against the wall, I had access to her every need. I considerately inserted a finger. It entered easily, indicating that she wanted more – that she could handle more. I slowly inserted a second finger, causing her to gasp in pleasure. Still, her body was asking for more so he inserted a third one, and then the fourth one until she was full – until her legs were having trouble holding her up. I was thrusting his hand with waves of water splashing over his arm enhancing all sounds. The water rolled over her clit, which was now throbbing for more.

I couldn't let her cum – not just yet. First, I needed to be inside of her. I needed to feel her body against his, feel her limbs shudder over him, feel her vagina squeeze to orgasm. Sarah turned around so she could support herself against the wall while I penetrated her from behind.

My thrusts were deep and focused as I held onto her hips as she shook. Slipping an arm around her thigh, I was close but I needed watch her to cum first. My pruned fingers made small, gentle circles around her clitoris. It was all she needed to send her over the edge.

Sarah gripped onto the tiles, trying not to slip as a wave of pleasure washed over her. Her screams echoed through the bathroom as her pussy thrust and squeezed and let go of all inhibitions. Her soaking hair covering her face, she gasped for air once her body stopped shaking.

Turning to face me, I couldn't help but have smile plastered on my face. My eyes sparkling in awe of her orgasm. I watched as Sarah grabbed my painfully hard cock in her hands:

"now it's your turn" he voice husky

I could barely contain myself, and after a few strokes, I spurted all over her stomach, letting my seed drip all the way into her pussy. As the water washed away all traces of me from her body, watched it disappear down the drain. Shutting off the water, Sarah turned to me"

"Make me dirty again?"

Fuck yes

Chapter 3

Sarah

Waking to the delicious aroma of coffee lingers in the air. I was sore in the best way, and I needed a shower. I was sweating from the immense heat he seemed to generate with his broad, muscular body that enveloped me. I had never felt so cherished, had never been so thoroughly consumed in my life. I stretched like a cat, slithered out. I feel every moment from last night in every part of my naked body. Satisfaction. That's the best word to describe how I feel. The other side of the bed is cold and I frown. I can't believe he left me. Rising from bed I padded my way to the smell of the coffee in the kitchen. I find flowers and a note.

Good Morning Baby. You were sleeping so peacefully and didn't want to wake you. Enjoy your day writing xo

I make a cup of coffee from the small coffee maker crawl back in bed to send a message to Matthew.

The bed is empty without you. Thank you for my caffeine fix. I love you,
S x

As I waited for Matthew's reply, I finished my coffee and rose to check on Katherine. Still sound a sleep. God we were lucky parents. Katherine had been the great baby sleep through the night from the first moment we brought her home and now that she was four, she still slept well and was an absolute delight the rest of the time.

Returning to the bedroom I check my phone and Matthew's reply.

I'm sorry that I had to leave early this morning

baby, but this meeting is with the new investor I told you about. I'll be home about 4pm, I've organised a sitter for Katherine for the night. Some much needed US time.

M x

Us time had been something we hadn't had in years. Maybe this is Matthew finally trying to make things the way the use to be, before Eden and Jeanette. But it wasn't them I wanted to remember it was they days when Matthew seemed to become a whole different person. When his alpha male came to the surface and he would show me over and over again that I was his.

I lay back on the bed thinking of the day I found Matthew in the garage leaning against his tool bench. The first day I saw my husbands possessive side The way that he kissed me and the way we made love right there on his tool bench in the garage.

It was hot.

I definitely want more of where that came from but there was something different about it that day. It was like he was trying to mark me as his. I slide my hand down my body to my already slick pussy, remembering how he had unzipped my skirt at the side and taking my underwear with one tug he let them float to the floor. His voice in my ear as it was that day..

"Your fuck gorgeous" his words sent a rush of desire through me unlike anything I've ever felt before—until his palm slides between my legs and cups me before dragging a single thick finger through my wetness. Matthew groaned. Pure male, husky.

"You're fucking drenched for me. Jesus."

His fingertip swirls my opening, teasing me. My thighs flex, and when he dips just barely inside, my inner walls clench, greedy and wanting to be filled. What is happening to me? I push myself against his hand, and for a moment, he fills me. His hand drops away, and a cool rush of air precedes a light slap to my pussy.

"Wha—"

"My greedy wife is getting ahead of herself. I'll give you what you need, but you'll take it my way."

When I exhale sharply, another firmer smack lands in the same spot. And then he grips my hips and flips me onto my back in a single movement. My head is still spinning from the abrupt change in position, but my eyes track him as he leaves the edge of the tool bench, moves toward the tool stand box, crouches low, and then returns. He kneels at the base of the metal bench, grips my knees, and pulls me so my ass is almost hanging off the edge and my stilettos are resting on his shoulders. I'm completely and utterly exposed to him, and uncertainty fills me for a breath. He lifts something, and in the dim light of the garage, zippy ties.

I don't have time to question, because within moments he ties my ankles to the legs of the bench.

"I thought we might celebrate our new car with a bottle of wine" he says picking up a glass I hadn't noticed. It can't of been there long as glass was still frosted. Matthew lifted the glass to my lips. Mmm crisp white Sauvignon Blanc. Matthew took a sip for himself kissed me again. The mix of cool wine and his hot mouth, furthering my need.

With a grin Matthew leant back, "would you like more wine Sarah?"

"Please" not quite a beg but a plea for more. I watched Matthew take the bottle expecting him to refill the empty wine glass instead crouches down his mouth inches from my sex. His breath hot against my skin.

Suddenly, chilly liquid hits me and trickles down . . .

into his mouth. He catches the wine on his tongue, lapping up my wetness at the same time. Oh my God. Oh my God. Pleasure spikes through me as he sucks and nips and licks until I can't help but lift my hips and buck against his mouth, wanting more and more of this sensation. He stills, the pulsing in my pussy stops, and he lifts his mouth away.

"Wh—"

"You're not going to come until I give you permission. I'm going to enjoy my appetiser first."

My nipples pucker, and arousal raises goosebumps along every inch of my skin.

"Okay," I whisper.

"Please don't stop. Please." I don't know who this senseless creature is who's begging her husband to keep lavishing on her lady bits, but I honestly don't care. I expect him to resume his actions, but he does something else, something completely unexpected.

His dark eyes are locked on mine as he continues to thrust in and out with his finger and lowers his mouth to my clit. And he feasts. I'm riding high on the wave toward orgasm when a second finger pushes inside me for a moment before sliding lower. I flinch against the foreign feeling as his fingertip circles the pucker of my ass. I open my mouth to protest, but the sensation falls *away and is replaced by his teeth nipping at my clit.*

A moan rips from my throat as an orgasm rips through my body.

When I blink my eyes open, he's standing over me. He must have cut the ties on my legs from bench, even though I didn't realise it. His belt is undone, his pants are unzipped, and his hand is wrapped around a giant cock.

In a swift move I was impaled on his cock. A low groan came from Matthew's throat.

"Your, fucking mine," he repeated over and over again as ploughed into me. My head was spinning at the side to Matthew I had never seen before until he places his thumb between us pressing on my clit sending me over the edge once more.

I could feel myself tighten as my fingers plunge in and out of my soaked pussy, images of Matthew sending me over the edge.

"Mummy" Katherines voice echoes through our closed bedroom door.

"Yes, baby girl, I'll be right out" I jump up quickly grabbing my robe and opening the door.

"Can we have pancakes for breakfast." she says grabbing my arm and tugging me towards the kitchen.

"Of course baby. You can have anything you want."

"Even ice cream on my pancakes?" excitement in her voice.

I laugh quietly to myself before nodding. Katherines grin is from ear to ear before climbing up on to the breakfast bar stool. A chime from my phone alerts me to another message.

I almost forgot. There is a dress hanging in my office that I want you to wear tonight and Sarah no underwear.

M   xo

My face heats when I read Matthews text. Placing the pancakes with berries and I cream in front of Katherine, I bee line it Matthews home office and sure enough a low cut wrap dress hang from the clothes hook with black six inch stiletto placed neatly below it. I wasn't sure what Matthew had planned but it looks like our marriage is getting a fresh start.

Love Games Trilogy

Chapter 4

Connor

God, what did I agree to. I had been in love with Sarah for years, since the Christmas party Matthew introduced her to our group of friends. She showed up at our local bar in a little sundress with black kitten heels, she was breathtaking. Her innocence only adding to her charm. She had no idea that she had been lead into the lions den so to speak. Each one of us not only Dom's at Highclere but every bit alpha outside of the club.

For all these years I'd been content on sitting on the sidelines because of my friendship with them and how much I could loose if it all went bust. Fuck, I even agreed to be Katherine's god father. I absolutely adore her too. I would lay down my wife for that beautiful little girl. But now Matthew wants me to seduce his wife.

WTF

I should have said no but it was my only chance and Matthew had opened the door to it. Now was my chance to be have it all. The family I have loved for so long and Matthew is handing it to me on a silver platter. Everything had been arranged,. Matthew had given me strict instruction on what he wanted but his parting words on the phone call had been what showed me the most.

"I need you mate. Fuck we need you for this. I know you will always do the right thing by Sarah"

******

The following evening, I watched from the upstair balcony as Matthew and Sarah entered Highclere's main dungeon floor. Watching her take in the walls a velvet red with dark handcrafted logs outlining each closed double door as they walked through. It was like seeing it for the first time all over again. I do love this place though, it was like the barnwood builders met Christian Grey's play room, only on steroids. With private VIP mezzanine and playrooms on the second level,

Highclere was known to be the most exclusive BSDM club in Australia. A place I liked to call home.

Sarah's eyes darted around taking it all in. Her innocence oozed from her as she took in each scene. Her breath visibly hitching and slight shiver as they made through. Matthew looks up and gives me the cue I'd been waiting for. Action time I tell myself.

As planned one of club owners Declan approaches Matthew and asks to have a word before Matthew points to the mezzanine asking Sarah to wait upstairs. Sarah merely nods and follows his instructions like a good submissive.

My heart begins to race as she ascends the stairs.

"Connor" she says in surprise. I wasn't sure it was shock that I would be here in Highclere or that we were completely alone up here.

"Hello sweetheart" I walk forward leaning down to kiss her cheek gentle. God she smelts fucking fantastic. Like strawberries and cream. A treat I definitely wanted to taste.

Sarah stared at me in confusion. "I.. I didn't realise you were a member here." Not quite a question more of a statement to me.

"I certainly am and have been for a very long time." I can't hide the amusement I voice.

"Oh"the way her cheeks pinked make cock jump to life.

"I'm a consenting adult Sarah and a BDSM club is the perfect way to live out my fantasies. Wouldn't you say?"

"Yes"God she is so fucking beautiful in her innocence. Placing my hand on her waist I lead her to the balcony overlooking the main floor before placing here between the balustrade and my body. Trapping her for my pleasure. Time to see how much innocent she really is.

"Sexy isn't it, everybody enjoying something different. Some like spankings. Others rope play, others like to share" I say pointing to all the different scenes. "What's your fantasy Sarah" lowing my hear my lips on the shell of her ear.

"I.. I can't tell you that Connor." Not that I needed a response her body already told me everything I needed to know.

"Sarah, you can and you will. What you don't seem to realise yet is that I am the one who can make all your wildest fantasies happen. I, little one will make sure of it."

"When did you become so direct?" she whispered.

"Sweetheart, I've always been like this. How do you think Matthew met me? It wasn't just our apprenticeship that brought us together. We new the moment we met that we were both Dom's"

Sarah's gasp was audible and her shiver just a the first hint that she knew our relationship just changed.

Placing my hand at her waist once more with a light tug of the wrap dress bow her dress fell apart. Revealing a body straight out of my wet dreams. High, full breasts tipped by hard pink nipples, a waist small enough to span with my hands, gently curving hips, and long, long legs. And between those legs, not even a hint of hair, just the smooth, bare mound of her pussy.

My dick is so hard it hurts. She pinkened even more, a flush appearing on her face and chest, and whatever self-control I still has almost evaporated. I touched her breast, flicked my thumb over her nipple, and watched her pupils expand, turning her blue eyes darker.

Such a beautiful submissive.

But she's not mine.

Control—that's what I need right now. Control and distance from her. My cock is like a spike in my jeans, my balls so full I feel like I could blow any second. I've never come so close to fucking a woman and then stopped. I've never denied myself something I wanted so badly.

Instead, I let her go. That was the deal.

Fuck

Despite my body's burning need, I couldn't bring myself to do it. I couldn't do that to her or Matthew.

The sound of a voice clearing behind Sarah, makes her jump.

Matthew. Great great fucking timing.

Pulling away and swiftly retying her dress, the look of horror on Sarah's face say it all. Matthew on the other hand had planned every moment to perfection. The slight smirk on his face while Sarah had her back turned to him told me that I had for filled my duties for the evening.

I can't help myself but have one last moment with her, before leaning forward and kissing her cheek. My hot breath against the shell of her ear.

"I believe someone is here for you little one." With a curt nod to Matthew, I leave the mezzanine and head down to dungeon floor and make my way to the privacy of Jackson's empty office.

Lifting my shirt and unzipping my jeans, I pull out my engorged cock and close my fist around it. Squeezing my eyes shut, I imagine that I'm inside her and it's her inner walls gripping my dick so tightly. Images of Sarah filling my mind, it takes less than a minute for me to come, my seed spurting across me my stomach.

Chapter 5

Sarah

"Matthew, I" I couldn't think of the words. I'm sorry wasn't enough. I'd let another man touch me. See my naked breasts.

"So, my precious wife likes to be touched by other men." I can practically hear his teeth gritting as he speaks.

"No. Yes. God Matthew I don't know. I'm so confused right now."

"Pleading insanity are you?"

"No" I said shaking my head.

"Well the my precious, you seem to be enjoying it. " he ran his knuckles softly down my heated cheek, his hand not stopping but continuing down the front of my lowly strapped wrap around dress.

"Your nipples are like tight little pebbles, did you enjoy it a he had his hand right here?" Matthew pulled the sash that held the dress together exposing my breasts again. As his hand gently grazed the round globes of my breast, I could feel my breath hitch. Matthew's eyes dilated and he seemed to grown taller, stronger, more dominate.

"Tell me Sarah, did he make you wet?" No accusation in he is voice, just certainty.

I couldn't deny it any long "Yes."

"Good girl, you didn't lie to me. Would you like Connor to touch your pussy?"

I stared at Matthew, is this what he wanted. To share me with another man? To share me with Connor?

"Don't lie to me Sarah, that would be braking the rules. Because here at Highclere it's all about trust, honest and being true to yourself and your Dom."

He let go of my nipple and asked, "Do you wish Connor was here...with us?"

"Oh, God!" The words escaped my lips before I could control them. Matthew had taken my other nipple between his lips and bit down gently, as his quiet question rolled around in my head.

Honestly, until he'd mentioned it, I hadn't been thinking about Connor at all, but now that he brought it up, the two of them here together, say...with one mouth on each of my nipples, was a thought so erotic, so forbidden, so very sinful, that just thinking about it, as he bit and sucked one nipple, while kneading my other breast with his hand, made me almost come against him in my dress.

"Together? Or separate? Spell it out for me, Matthew. I'm not exactly thinking logically right now. Maybe we should stop..." I panted.

"Oh no, not unless you really want me to. You're close, aren't you? Just the idea of the two of us, Connor and I both, pleasuring you between us, is enough to send you over the edge, isn't it?"

"Yes" my head lolled. "Please, Mathew Please" I beg.

Chapter 5

Matthew

Watching Sarah with Connor was fucking hot and I could see instantly that she wanted him too.

"If a call Connor back up here and ask him to fuck that tight little pussy of yours, you won't object?"

"No, Yes" she whined.

"Your still not being honest with me Sarah" I lead her across to the leacher sofa. " You broke the rules, Sarah"

"Are you going to punish me?"

She tried to make her voice whinier than normal—which sounded pretty comical.

"Should I put my clothes on and we leave?"

"Oh, you're not going anywhere." I reached over and grabbed her wrist. "But I am going to give you a spanking."

"Wait!" She squirmed in my grasp as I pulled her over my knees and put a little pressure on her back so that she couldn't move.

"Such a naughty wife…" I traced the back of her thighs and the curve of her ass.

"You knew the rules."

"I did…" She sighed and stopped struggling when she felt my touch.

"You chose to break them." I moved my hand to the other side of her ass and traced down her thigh.

"I can't deny that." I felt goosebumps forming underneath my touch.

"Now I have to punish you." I pulled my finger away and cupped her ass.

"Fine—just one." God, she was a complete brat. She lifted her ass up against my hand.

"I think this deserves more than one." I teased her by sliding forward and gently stroking her pussy.

"Two?" She moaned and looked over her shoulder at me.

"I was thinking ten." I pulled my finger away.

"That's too many…" She shook her head and groaned.

"It's' been years since you spanked me."

"Well, I certainly don't think you're going to learn your lesson with two and maybe I should be spanking you more often so you remember the rules " I narrowed my eyes and chuckled.

"Fine…" She groaned again—but there was a hint of playfulness, and she rubbed her ass against my hand.

"Ten it is."

That seems more appropriate." I lifted my hand and brought it down on the right side of her ass.

SMACK!

"That's one." She dropped her head and giggled.

"You don't have to count them." I pulled my hand back and gave her two quick ones—the second landed on the left side of her ass, and the other landed in the same spot as the first. SMACK! SMACK!

"Ow…"

She winced as the third one landed, but she wiggled her ass and pressed it against my hand. "Are you beginning to learn your lesson?" I pulled my hand back.

SMACK! SMACK! SMACK!

"Matthew…" She exhaled sharply.

SMACK! SMACK! SMACK! SMACK!

I let my hand stay where the last one landed as I watched the slickness from Sarah's folds drip down my pant leg. Fuck. My wife was getting of on this as much as I was.

Chapter 7

Connor

I'd cleaned myself up and returned to the dungeon floor. I needed a drink and there was nothing stopping me from getting drunk as I had no intentions to play tonight, with anyone after what had happened with Sarah.

With a light buzz to my head and wondering the dungeon floor, flopping down into the leather sofas opposite Jackson and his two subs for the night. I swear he'd been acting like a complete manwhore the last few months. As the hours pass by Jackson sends sub after sub to try and entice me to play.

"Jackson, how many fucking times do I need to tell you I'm not interested?"

As much as I loved my mate and resident Dom

at Highclere Jackson, sometimes he could be a complete jackass. I've been dogging willing subs all night long, and coming up with creative reasons why I wasn't interested. What was supposed to be a night with Sarah was turning into anything but.

Up until a yesterday, this was my life. Now I felt slightly out of place, like I didn't belong here. The hot, leggy blonde who spent the last hour grabbing my inner thigh and asking me if she could suck me off, didn't even tempt me.

"Yeah, I heard you loud and clear, seeing that you've been checking your damn phone all night and ignoring the parade of pussy I've brought to our table." He smirked and threw the rest of his drink back in one gulp. "Since when did you grow a vagina?"

The two subs he had sitting on each leg chuckled. The blonde was running her long red painted fingernails along his chest, while the other had her hand resting between his legs.

I looked away, trying to smother my frustration. I had to remind myself he was younger than me, in the Royal Australian Navy and in his prime. Women ate that shit up, a man in a uniform or some crap.

He deserved his time as Navy life had been hard on him and sooner or later nights like this would become a distant memory. I kind of felt sorry for his stupid ass, but at the same time, I was glad he was enjoying the thrill of it all. Rolling my neck from side to side, I sat back in my chair and crossed my legs.

"Watch it, Jackson," I warned playfully.

"I know how much money went into fixing that mouth of yours. You're about two seconds away from losing a couple more teeth if you don't keep your trap shut. I would hate for you not to be able to use it tonight."

Jackson let out a loud laugh.

"Good thing I don't need to use my mouth to get the job done." He winked and slightly adjusted his knees to better support his two subs for the night.

Looking at Jackson for the approval to speak "You know," the blonde spoke up, "if you don't mind sharing, there is enough love for both of you." She glanced between Jackson and me, with her partner's head nodding in approval. I shook my head with a laugh.

"I appreciate the offer. But I'm good."

"You sure, Sir?" She looked me over with a gleam in her eye. "I know we can make it worth your while."

"Sweetheart, no offence, but I'm really not interested."

She looked at me as if I'd sprouted a second head. "Well, that's a first. You must be gay. My bad."

Jackson almost fell off the chair from laughing so hard. The girls had no choice but to jump off or risk landing on their asses. I sat up in my seat and squared my shoulders. This sub was pissing me off. I took a sip of my drink and connected my gaze to hers.

"I can assure you that I'm not gay. I guess I just prefer my 'sub' to not throw herself at me like a hooker needing a fix."

I gave her a once-over and noticed the scowl form on her face. It looked tight like she'd just had a Botox injection. I was surprised her facial muscles even moved.

"Fuck you, asshole." She spat out, tossing her drink in my direction and stormed off. Her friend quickly ran after her. Jackson was still laughing as they both sulked away. They only made it a couple booths down before they found another couple of well-dressed Doms at least ten years older than us. Clearly these two subs had gotten over their heartbreak and were off looking for their next round of free drinks.

"Sorry, mate; I didn't mean to fuck up your night and chase off your subs."

Chapter 8

Sarah

The morning by in flash, Matthew had left for a morning meeting with investors and I dropped Katherine off to her sitter so I could get some writing done. There was no mention from Matthew as to what had happed at Highclere last night.

Sighing, I finally closed my laptop, rubbing at my eyes. standing up, feeling disconcerted. I had barely gotten any writing done. It seemed like it should be later than it was. I couldn't go to sleep and I wasn't even remotely tired. I walked over to the window and stared out over the Melbourne skyline. Suddenly, our penthouse apartment felt claustrophobic. I couldn't seem to get away from my thoughts. I knew that it was wrong. I love

Matthew but thoughts of Connor crept in.

His touch. The warmth of his breath on my ear. The way I seemed to fit perfectly in his sculpted arms as we looked out over Highclere's dungeon floor. Heat swirled in my core.

I grabbed my keys and shoved them into my pocket. Then I grabbed my jacket. I just needed to get some fresh air. A little drive around downtown would do me good. Or at least, it wouldn't make me think about anything that I wasn't already thinking about.

Connor.

******

I know I shouldn't do this without telling Matthew but I can't not be honest with Connor and myself. Thank goodness all these years of of being friends with Connor it only took me fifteen minutes to get to Connor's suburbs home.

As I stand in the rain staring at the car parked in his driveway I try to work up the courage to knock on the door. What if he isn't home? What if he has someone with him? Would that be a bad thing? The longer I stood the more butterflies I had. Taking a few tentative steps towards the porch, the light flicks on and the door opens.

"Sarah" his deep voice filled with surprise.

I open my mouth to speak but no words come out. He's divine, white tee stretched across his broad shoulders, faded black jeans sitting low on his hips, his hair tousled as if he'd spend the night running his hands throughout in frustration.

"Sarah, are you going to continue standing in the rain or come in?" his voice filled with jest.

I look down at myself. I'm soaked. My clothes clinging to every curve. Looking up at Connor, I take the few tentative steps up the porch and to the door and cross the threshold. Taking me by the hand "Come lets get you dry"he leads me through the house.

Connor's touch was intoxicating. His hand firmly held mine, interlacing our fingers as I took in the kitchen, astonished at the similarly impersonal yet beautiful atmosphere of the room. The cabinets alone had to be worth a fortune, with expensive-looking wood accompanied by stainless steel appliances so shiny that I could have sworn they were never used.

He stopped me in front of the standalone island, giving my hand a squeeze before letting go.

Connor walks from the room returning with a large fluffy towel. Rater than passing me the towel to my outstretched hand he walks behind me taking the towel and slowly and methodically drying my hair. His hands never touching me only the towel. Connor works his way down my body before wrapping me in the towel.

"Let's get a drink and talk."

A drink was exactly what I needed. I watched as Connor poured the ruby red wine from the decanter on the counter. He poured another glass and handed it to me. Drinking it down in three gulps.

"Need another?" asks with a smirk on his face.

"Please." A feeling of desperation filled me as he refilled the glass, and I took a small sip.

"Look, I know I've already messed up. Is this because of the other night? Do you feel guilty for what happened? You shouldn't, it wasn't your fault. I–"

"No, Sarah." Connor took a long sip of his drink as he stared at me.

Connor placed his drink down on the marble countertop and then set mine next to his, grabbing my hands and forcing me to look him in the eyes again.

"What if I told you, Sarah, I wanted you, as my —" he stopped, his tongue flicking out across his lips. Instantly I could feel myself drawing closer, following the scent of wine. My heart beat faster as his thumbs gently drew circles on the back of my hands.

"There isn't anyone else I wanted like I did you that night in the club."

"Why?" Her question lingered in the arias I scrambled to get my thoughts together to explain that I had been in love with her for years.

Chapter 9

Connor

Fuck

I hadn't expected to find Sarah standing in the rain on my doorstep. I saw her through the window as I passed on my way upstairs. So beautiful standing there absolutely soaking wet every delicious curve of her body outlined, her nipples clearly visible beneath her cotton dress. As if she wasn't permanently etched into my memory already, she certainly was now.

Adjusting my hardened cock in my pants, I flick on the porch light and open the front door. My breath hitches as she takes the few steps towards my door, I can't help myself I have to touch her. Grabbing her by the hand, I lead her through the door and towards the kitchen even though every cell in body wants to take her upstairs and explore every inch of her. I had to stop these thoughts as my cock was already aching and if I got any hards my pant zipper would bust open.

Placing the second glass of wine in from of Sarah , I knew she was using it dutch courage as the words "why" leave her lips. Lips I wanted to taste.

"The list is pretty long Sarah, where do you want me to start" I round the bench with my glass in hand. I brought my free hand up to her mouth and ran my thumb along her bottom lip.

"Because your the most beautiful, kind and loving person I know. Because the day I meet you, I knew that I had to have you in my life in anyway I possibly could. Sarah, I knew I loved you then as I do now and always have done. Why do you think you have never seen me with any other women in my life?"

"Ohh" her lips form a perfect 'O'. Lowering my head I could no long hold back what I felt like I had waited a life time for. My lips touching hers. Fuck she tasted like heaven. Hell yes this what I'd been wanting all my life. My nostrils flared as her breath grew harsh. She crushed her lips to mine, breathing me in as she kissed me.

Her mouth even softer than I'd fantasied about, with the perfect amount of tongue and lip, I moaned into her mouth. I ran my fingers through her hair, with just the right amount of press against her scalp. Sarah shuddered, moaning and driving forward into my mouth.

Hating to have to pull back, I knew I had to because if I didn't it would be a mistake that neither of us were ready for.

"We got caught up in the moment," I whispered pulling away. "But I'm a patient man, Sarah. Especially when it comes to getting something I want. And you're not just something I want, but you're also worth the wait."

Every impulse in my body wanted to lay her down on the marble counter top and show her how good we could be together, but I needed to keep a level head here. She wasn't just a random fuck, and for the first time in my life, I wasn't sure how to handle a woman. Normally, it was just about the sexual conquest, but with Sarah, it was so much more than that. Her stare never wavered from mine.

"Thank you for being patient with me." She

leaned in and brushed the softest kiss against my mouth. "And for making me feel better.'

A laugh slipped out of me.

"Sweetheart, we stopped way too short of the many things that I am capable of doing to make you feel better," I said teasingly.

She brought her head down to my shoulder. A protectiveness swept over me, and my heart began to pound erratically in my chest.

"I don't know what it is about you, but there's something happening between us. I know you feel it." I exhaled deeply. The truth was, I knew all the reasons why this shouldn't be happening, but I've never felt anything like this before.

*****

What the hell was wrong with me? Sarah was beautiful. A wet dream on legs. Most of all, she wanted me. She was submitting to me. And I couldn't do it. I'd sent Sarah home to her husband.

When the sound of a door closed, I dropped my head into my hands. Her scent wafted into my nose. It was everywhere. On my tongue. My lips. I could feel her. Taste her. Smell her. And I kicked her out. Why?

Chapter 10

Matthew

I hadn't planned to stop by Connor's but thought it would be better have the conversation in person than over text or email. Now I had to find the words to tell my longtime friend that I simply couldn't share my wife. Sarah is mine and mine alone.

Shaking my head I mentally kick myself as I'm the reason we were in this situation in the first place but I thought maybe just maybe it would get Sarah an I back to what were before Eden and Jeanette almost taken our lives.

As pulled the car into his street Sarah's car sat directly in-front of Connor's two-story craftsman. I watched as Sarah take his hand and follow Connor inside my heart sank. Sarah wanted Connor.

My chest was still tight from the anxiety and frustration from seeing Sarah being lead into Connor's home. It was the exact opposite of what I had planned, and things had taken a turn for the worse, if that were even possible. Everything we had together. Everything we had worked for after Eden and Jeanette, was over. I looked at myself in the mirror as I undid the button on my collar.

"Sarah, what have you done to us?"

I shook my head as frustration turned to sadness. The lump in my throat made it difficult to swallow. I stretched my neck, willing the sadness to go away, but it didn't help. It was overwhelming. I reached for the bottle of Calvin Klein cologne and sprayed it and then fought the urge to hurl it across the bathroom.

"Fuck!"

Gripping the edge of the granite sink, I took a cold, hard stare at myself as I clenched my jaw. My chest expanded as a slow, deep breath filled my lungs and I slowly exhaled. I needed to focus. I needed to get to work and distract myself.

******

Hours later the sound of the front doors clicked

open. Sarah entered carrying our sleeping daughter. She must have collected her from the sitters on the way back from Connor's. Taking Katherine from her arms, I carry her through to her bed before tucking her in. Stepping back into the main lounge of our apartment, the sound of the smack and the sting of her hand hitting my face were almost simultaneous.

"You're a jerk!" she yelled as she stepped across the threshold.

"What The Fuck, Sarah" I backed away, unsure whether she would strike again. She reared her hand back again and then brought it to my face. Instinctively I raised mine to block it, but her movements were much slower and more deliberated. This wasn't another slap. Her hands cupped my face. Sarah brought her face close to mine and I resisted the urge to move. I wasn't sure if I wanted to move toward her, or away. Then her mouth closed over mine as she forcefully kissed me. The faint taste of iron filled my mouth as I realised I must have bitten my cheek when she slapped me. Blood.

"You went to his house"

"I didn't sleep with Connor. I turned him down.

He wanted me to be his sub, to me with you. But it's not what I want."

I stared into her eyes as I ran my tongue against the sore spot on my left cheek. I wiped my mouth with my hand, looking for blood, but only seeing the faintest tinge.

"Nothing happened. I couldn't do that to you."

"Maybe I should have fucked him. That's what you want isn't it?" She screamed at me. "You love to share your women, don't you Matthew. You like to have a woman all twisted up over you and your mates. This time it's Connor. Did you think what this would do to me?"

"To our family?"

"To Connor?"

Her frustration growing as I just stood not saying a word. My hands in his pocket, my body stiff and my jaw set like stone.

"You told me no at highclere? You had to slap me?"

"I slapped you because you did this. You put me in a position I never wanted to be in."

I stood stunned. This wasn't how it was supposed happen. Was this the end of our marriage?

She looked at me as the tears fell. "So that's it. You are just going to stand there and say nothing. You're just giving up on us? After everything we shared, all the promises we've made, you're just going to walk away?" Her voice trembled. "I don't want to lose you, but I can't keep letting you push me away. All I want is to be with you. I've told you this a thousand times, but I can't force you to believe me. I can't keep doing this."

She pulled her hand from mine. "I'm the only one fighting for us."

As she looked away, and something shifted; I could feel it, and it made me sick to my stomach. "I'm not going to put life on hold anymore." her voice small. I watched as Sarah turned and left. I wasn't sure where she was going or if she would ever come back to me.

Chapter 11

Sarah

I wasn't sure what I was doing but I knew that tonight I couldn't stay at home with Matthew. As I made my way through the streets of Melbourne I couldn't help but think about the night had been. My fight with Matthew but more so Connor. Pulling into the carpark of Mount Dandenong I realised I'd driven further than I thought. My skin heated as I remembered Connors lips on mine.

"Good." Leaning down, he fit his mouth over mine, and I did nothing to stop him. If anything, I leaned into that kiss and opened under him, giving into the desire of knowing what it would be like to kiss him. I was not disappointed.

Pulling my head back by my hair, he deepened the

kiss and stepped between my legs. The pressure of his body against mine made my nerve-endings sing as his tongue stroked against mine.

My mind spun out-of-control as his fingers danced down my spine and tugged at my shirt. When he broke off the kiss, his lips moved down my throat as his touch found bare skin beneath my shirt and caressed my back.

"Christ, Sarah, I could fuck you right here and now," he moaned as he ground against me.

Suddenly, I wished that that was nothing between us and feel his hard cock against my aching pussy. Fisting his shirt in my hands, I whimpered and pulled him back down for another kiss.

Rough.

Urgent.

All logical thought fled under his touch and demand, but before I could tell him that I was his, he backed away.

"As much as I want you, now is not the time or place," he whispered with regret.

Blinking, I stared at him.

"Because Sarah, I won't hurt you by hurting Matthew. I know you still love him. When I fuck you for the first time, Sarah, there's going to be no hesitation on your part and no doubt."

" Please tell me that this is not some Sinful Game

you're trying to play with me by saying no."

Oh, sweetheart, this is no game for me. This is what I want but not like this."

My phone buzzes beside me bringing me out of my daydream. Looking at the text I mentally kick myself. While I'd been having my own pity party I'd forgotten to send through the new edits to Kallee my publisher.

Hey Sarah, just wondering what time you were going to send through those edits. As I'd love to get them to the beta group by the morning. K

Shit , sorry. Time got away from me I'll send them through in 30. S

Chapter 12

Matthew

Sarah returned last night but it was hours after she had stormed out. I listened as she sat at her laptop thing til the we hours of the morning. I couldn't go to her. I had done this to us.

It didn't surprise me when I woke to an empty bed this morning. Sarah must have slept in Katherine's room or maybe the guest room. With no other choice I got up and went about my morning routine. Shaving, showering, and breakfast. I was miserable.

As the day wore on and I wrapped up the first meeting that got virtually nothing accomplished, I checked my phone for the umpteenth time, hoping to see something from her.

A missed phone call.

A text.

I would have even taken a fuck you, if it meant that I knew she was thinking of me. All I could see was that look on her face when I'd lashed out at her. Knowing that it was the last thing I said to her was tearing me up inside.

Chapter 13

Sarah

I wake up earlier than usual probably because I wasn't in my own bed. As I go to sit up the gurgling in my stomach rising into my chest and lodging itself in my throat. I have to throw the covers off and make a mad dash to the bathroom. Luckily, I make it in time to spill my guts into the toilet. A vile acidity fills my mouth, coats my tongue. I stare in dismay at the murky toilet water, both fascinated and disgusted by the bits and pieces of last night's dinner floating there. It had to be from the stress of everything that was going on. Stuck between my husband and the man I had grown to love over the years and only now seeing that he means more than I ever thought possible. I had to fix this. I had too or I would lose them both.

There was only one thing to do, tell them the truth. Matthew was already at home in his office, so I had to convince Connor to see me.

Can you come to the penthouse, we need to talk? S

I'd come anywhere for youuuuu C x

? S

I doon't think I should dirve though. C x

Are you drunk? S

No, well maybeeee. C

Where are you? S

Highclereeeeee C

The feeling of jealousy and shame shot through

my body. I'd never heard him speak like that. Was he drunk because of me? Was he with someone else already? Nope. I can this right now. I need him here. I can't hide this any longer.

I'll send a car over to get you. Please drink the coffee they bring. I need you to do this for me. S

K, for yu. C xoxoxoxoo

****

I watched him as he walked toward the double doors. He didn't look drunk, despite being a little rough around the edges. I hoped that meant he was going to listen to me when I told him what to do. He didn't give me the impression that he was a man who was accustomed to taking orders, much less obeying them. In fact, the way he carried himself made me think that not many people bossed him around, not without repercussions of some kind.

Something low in me throbbed at the thoughts of rewards and punishment, but I didn't let it linger. As the doors closed Matthew appears from his office.

"What the fuck is he doing here?" He scowled.

"I'm here for Sarah, you dickhead." Connor spat . "She said she need to talk so I'm here"

They both turned to look at me.

I opened my mouth and closed it. It felt like the air had been sucked out of the room. My brain frantically searched for a way to redeem myself, tried to find words that would be good enough to get me out of this mess. There was so much to explain, and the pressure of being put on the spot had my thoughts all jumbled up.

Matthew started to speak and then stopped. The look that came over his face is one I'll never forget.

"Matthew."

I felt like I was grasping at straws while trying to find a way to calm the situation. "I can explain."

Matthew got right up in my face. "If you have any explaining to do, it's to me. Not him. Now, start talking." Connor shoved him back, his temper rising to the surface.

"Don't fucking talk to her like that."

"Matthew!" I reached for his hand to calm him

down. All the fears and the angst I'd been feeling these past few weeks came flooding forward. I stood before both men, and I didn't know what do, what to say, or how to fix this. There was no way to rewind the clock. No matter how much I wanted to.

So, there I stood wondering how the hell I let any of this happen. Just an hour ago, all I had to worry about was getting through my next novel. Now, I had to worry about how I was going to get us out of this mess. How I was going to explain all this to my daughter.

Tears burned the back of my eyes when I thought about what this would mean for all of us. I wanted to wrap my arms around Matthew and beg him to take me away from this nightmare. The thought of losing him cracked my heart wide open, and I knew if he left me, there would be no way to fix it.

My eyes shifted to the man on my right. We loved each other once, but somewhere along the way, we lost each other too. There was so much history between us, and because of Katherine we'll always be connected, but that's where it stopped. I might have done the wrong thing for the right reasons, but I'm not sure any excuse I could give Connor would make a difference. What I could give him was the truth. My throat goes dry as I fight the tears that continued to fall.

"I'm in love with you, Connor. I'm in love with you both."

His breath hitched, and the look on his face shattered me.

"Sarah?" I could see the torment in Matthew's eyes as he waited for me to answer. Regret stirred between us as the fallout from my actions came crashing down around me. My shoulders sagged in defeat. "I'm so sorry. This wasn't how I meant for this to come out. I know I have a lot of explaining to do to the both of you. Please just hear me out."

"Matthew, I didn't mean…" I trail off as he turns hard eyes on me, his expression totally closed off again. I try again, "It's not that I… Shit." I give up. Matthew isn't giving me an inch, and I don't know what to say, anyway. I will always want him. It's just that I wanted Connor, too. And I'm so fucking tired of feeling bad about what I want. I throw my hands up in the air, exasperated.

"I just didn't want this to be complicated!" Matthew's lips tighten into a thin line, but Connor laughs.

"I mean, it doesn't seem all that complicated to me," Connor says, smiling at me warmly before his eyes move over to Matthew. Connor looks him over slowly, and even watching it, his gaze feels like molten honey to me, lingering on that mouthwatering erection that—despite Matthew's angry scowl and closed-off expression—is still at full mast.

God, Matthew wears suits like nobody's business, and this one looks particularly sexy against that strong, lean body. I have no doubt that my own expression matches Connor's at this point, but I only realise it when Matthew looks back and forth between the two of us, swallowing hard as his scowl turns to a sexy brand of confusion.

"What?" he manages, crossing his arms as if he can shield himself from both of us.

Connor looks over at me, the same warm heat I'd seen in Highclere flaring in his eyes. "Not complicated from where I'm standing, Matthew," he says. "I mean, hell. There is nothing I have fucking wanted more in my life."

I suck in a sharp breath as his words do something wicked to me. Both men at once… I bite my lip, stifling a moan. So hot. Matthew makes a small sound, and my eyes snap to his. His confusion has turned into something close to terror. He shakes his head, holding up his hands in front of him.

"Jesus fuck, Connor!" he shouts.

Connor's open expression suddenly goes dark. It might be the first time in my life I've ever seen him looking anything other than easygoing and relaxed.

"Matthew, I've never hidden my feelings for Sarah. If you can't handle it, get over it, because it's clear that Sarah wants this too and we don't have time for hiding who we are or our feelings bullshit anymore."

Suddenly, I'm struck by another wave of nausea. I looking up them both.

"Sarah" they say in unison.

Turning on a dime, I run into the ensuite bathroom and gagging again, leaning miserably against the toilet bowl. Yep, they were definitely going to find out what was going on with me. It was only a matter of time.

Chapter 14

Matthew

I listened as Sarah heaved into the toilet yet again. The look on Connor's face told me he was worried about her as much as I was. Last time she had been this sick was when Jeanette had poisoned her and she had miscarried. I called the doctor without any hesitation. The man promised to be over as soon as possible—one of the perks of having money: doctors who made house calls at a moment's notice. I then went into the bathroom and helped Sarah to her feet.

"You should rest," Connor said, nudging her toward the bed. She shook her head.

"I'm fine," she insisted, much as she had the day before. "I'd love a cup of peppermint tea, though."

"Sure," I said, "as long as you'll take it easy." I nudged her toward the bed again before heading off to the kitchen. Connor sat holding her on the bed. Twenty agonising minutes later the door bell chimed. Tanking the doctor I lead him through to our bedroom where Sarah lay resting.

"Mrs Davidson," the doctor said, nodding curtly at her. "What can I help you with today?"

She seemed nervous, and she fidgeted with her sleeves, biting her lower lip.

"I think I'm pregnant," she said quietly. Her eyes darted toward my face and then quickly away from me. I felt as though the floor had dropped out from under me. I could hardly believe what I had just heard. Sarah was pregnant again? I spared a look at her stomach, but she wasn't showing yet. She couldn't be too far along.

For one brief moment, I was elated. Another baby.

But then, as her words sunk in, a sick feeling rose in my stomach. Had Sarah lied to me after all and slept with Connor and this was Connors baby?

The look on Connor's face mirrored mine. Pure shock. Without missing a beat his gentle lifted Sarah from his arms and stalked towards the hall. I wanted to kill him. Leaving Sarah in the capable hands of the doctor I chased after him. Connor stopping halfway down the hall and grabbing me as I lunged for him and slamming me agains the wall.

"Before you fucking start, I never fucked her." his face a married with pain and sadness.

Fuck

"I wanted to, fuck Matthew, I love Sarah more than life itself but I couldn't. I couldn't do it to you. So, I decided the only way I could have her was with you, not because of you."

This is so fucking stupid.

A smile stretches across my lips, worry and pain and all things awful about the last week melting away. I placed my hand on top of Connor's grip on my shirt.

"Then I guess the answer to all our problems is that she needs us both." I smile.

Connor's grip loosens and he sets me back on my feet.

"Is that what you truly want mate, because if we do this its for life, no backing out" he asks stepping back.

"I can't think of anyone I would rather share

my family with than you." Putting my hand out hoping that Connor will shake it and act of peace making.

"Daddy, what are doing?" Katherine asks rounding the corner and rubbing her sleepy eyes.

Connor looks from me to Katherine before bending down to lift her up.

"Sweetheart, your daddy was just asking me if I wanted to become your daddy too?"

The excitement on Katherine's face was heartwarming. "Really, I can have two daddies? Please Connor be my daddy too. Please."

"Sweetheart, anything for you." Connor kissed Katherine's forehead before carrying her down the hall to her bedroom. Letting out a sigh of relief, I spilled to myself. It looked like it was going to be alright after all.

Chapter 15

Sarah

The doctor left after giving me an injection of Metoclopramide for the vomiting Both Connor and Matthew slicked into the bedroom. None of the supporting black eyes so it was a good start. Matthew stepped forward "Sarah, I'm sorry" his apology momentarily shocking me.

"Sarah" Connor continued "we love you and don't want you to choose between us. We" turning his head to look at Matthew.

"Baby, if you still want us both. We want you too. Together" Matthew

"I don't know how this—" I flutter my hands up and down, indicating both of them, all three of us.

"I don't know how this is supposed to work; I

never thought this would be my life."

I bite my lip, joy that the fact that this is my life sending sparkles through me, points of light that war with the darkness of my fear.

"But I do know that I want this to work, I want us to work. And I want—"

Matthew had gone to Connor. I don't know how or where; they wouldn't say. But it doesn't matter. My heart's finally beating at a regular speed again now that I know his what they both want. I made way up from the bed as hunger finally decided to rear it hears. As I made us all grilled cheese sandwiches, and Connor and I listened to Matthew apologise profusely about how he handled everything.

I'm just glad that we could all agree that this is what we wanted. That this the life and home we wanted. That's the crux of it, right? The idea of the three of us, together, all at once, making a home, making a life. It's so overwhelming, and yet... it feels right. I continue, swallowing my fear and letting that joy continue to spread through my body.

Oh, God, I can't believe I'm going to do this.

Chapter 16

Connor

One month later

"Fuck me, Connor," she whispers, wrapping her arms around my neck and pulling herself flush with my body. Those amazing breasts flatten against my chest and her legs tighten around me and her heat, her core, that sweet, sweet pussy I can taste on my own lips, connects at the perfect angle...

"Oh, fuuuuuuuuuuck, Sarah," I groan, pushing inside her, going deep into her tight, wet heat as I crush my mouth against hers, swallowing more of those delicious sounds she's been giving me all night. And... holy fucking shit. I'm balls deep, and she feels amazing.

Feels like heaven. Feels better than I could ever

describe. I'm done with slow.

Just can't anymore, and she doesn't want it. I pull back and thrust in hard, and then I do it again. And then again. We're moving together, immediately in sync, and it's exactly like my fantasy, but a billion times better. It's fucking perfect. " who would have thought that having Matthew watch Sarah and I have sex would be so fucking hot.

"You two look so good," Matthew pants.

"Look at Sarah, Connor, look how amazing you're making her feel, look how much she fucking loves your cock."

My balls start to tighten up as I listen to him. Christ. When I look over—oh fucking God—his eyes are hooded and his face flushed and his hand jerking hard and fast over his cock.

"Oh God, Matthew," Sarah moans, her heels spurring me on, digging into my ass.

"You… you… like this?"

"You're incredible, Sarah," he grits out.

"So fucking sexy. Connor looks so good, buried inside you. How does it feel?" Her nails score my back, and her incredible body starts to tighten all around me. She moans, and I know she can't answer him. I can't, either.

But oh please, oh fucking please, I want to hear it. Want to hear him urging us on. Getting off on it. Knowing that this is what Matthew wants too.

"She's about to come," he pants, making me groan.

"Her thighs are shaking, Connor. God, fuck her harder She's loving it. You're loving it, Sarah, aren't you? Connor, fuck… fuck… do it. Come for him. Sarah."

Neither one of us have wanted to say no to him, not all night. Not when he's the one that's giving us all what we need. Telling us it's okay to want what we want. This is no different. Sarah cries out, a stuttering, shuddering wail that strokes every fucking cell in my body.

Chapter 17

Sarah

It was the first time we had returned to Highclere since Matthew, Connor and I had decided to make our manège a permeant fixture in our lives. Connor had given me his training Connor since he still had Masters rights at Highclere. It as intoxicating every time they placed it around my neck. Even more so, seeing the dominant side of them in full flight sent every part off me tingling.

Watching them as they approached, I held my breath. Everything stood still as together they commanded my attention. I had an urge to spear my hands into their perfectly coiffed hair and kiss them, but I resisted, allowing them to control the situation. Within his own private room of Highclere, I could submit to whatever carnal pleasures they wanted. Connor brushed the back of his knuckles against my cheek and my eyes lit up. Seconds seemed like hours as she waited for them to take me. Matthews strong hand slid around my waist, and I released a sigh, my eyes never leaving his.

"I think it's time baby."

My heart flipped as he leaned to kiss e. Tasting scotch on his tongue, I opened to him returning his passionate kiss. Without ending my kiss with Connor, Matthew's hand slipped through the slit of my dress and cupping my bare mound, I moaned.

"We want everything tonight, Sarah." Connor spoke into my mouth, caressing my lips with his own.

"Your body. Your heart." Matthew continued.

Breathless, I could only give a small moan in acknowledgement. My knees faltered as he fingered my tiny pearl of my swollen clit tingling in arousal.

"Hmm….you like this, don't you?"

"Oh my God…"

"I love how responsive you are, my sweet wife."

I cried his Matthew's name as he pumped his middle finger into my pussy, his thumb continuing its erotic assault on my clitoris. I dug my fingers into Connor's forearm, and my forehead falling to his chest, as I heaved for breath.

"Do you have any idea what you've do to us?" Matthew moved behind me and ground his against the peak of my ass.

"How important you are to us?" Connor murmured as he kissed his way down my neck.

"Please."

"That's right, sweetheart. Beg us, because you're all ours. You'll always be our"

"Please" Sarah choked out.

I tensed in desire as Matthew slid another digit into her, curling it inside her sensitive channel. As Matthew's hand glided underneath the fabric and cupped her bare breast, I came undone. With fingers deep inside me, I clenched around them, spasming in pleasure.

"Please, yes…I'm coming…" I sucked for air as I came down, surprised as Matthew withdrew his fingers and inserted them into her lips.

"Couch," Matthew ordered.

Disoriented, I allowed them to bend me over its soft fluffy arm rest. Connor settled a pillow underneath my head and as Matthew promptly lifted the back of my dress. A rush of cold air brushed over my exposed pussy and I spread my legs wider to accept him. His palm lifted and I went to lift upward. Her effort was met with a firm slap on her arse.

"Stay. No moving." His commanding voice wrapped around me, and I did as I was told. The sound of running water and a drawer opening drew her attention and her heart raced. A warm hand caressed her bottom and I breathed in delight. I turned her head, her eyes meeting his.

"Do you know how much you mean to us, Sarah?" he asked, unzipping his pants.

"Our lives are nothing without you."

"Please… I need you both." It was all I could manage. His palm brushed over both my cheeks, Matthew's crown prodding my entrance. I'd go insane from the lingering anticipation as Connor positioned himself at my mouth. Licking my lip all I could do is beg again.

"Please…"

I was almost salivating by the time he reached me. I needed to taste him, hell, I ached to taste him. I slid the tip of him over my tongue and licked him like the sweetest ice cream I'd ever tasted. The moan above my head drove me on, feeding the fire. I wrapped my hand around the girth of him, and aimed him where I wanted him. I kept teasing him, at first, before drawing him deeper and taking what I needed from him as I gave to him as well. I bobbed my head, taking him deep and then pulling him out, looking up at him.

"We need you, too," Matthew told me, sheathing inside me.

"More than you know." Connor added.

"Ahhh…" I hummed along Connor's cock as Matthew entered me again. I shivered as my core fisted him. I'd come within minutes, and I did send Matthew and Connor over the edge with me.

"Don't think we are done with you yet Sweetheart" Connor says pushing back my now mangled mess of hair and stepping back.

"Oh baby, we are just getting started." Matthew says as leans forward kissing my shoulder before stepping back and lifting me to my feet. Taking me by the hand Connor pulls me into a heated kiss before turning and padding his way down the penthouse hall to Matthew and my bedroom. Matthew turns and kisses me just as hot and passionate as the one I had moments ago with Connor.

"Are you ready for more, baby?"

"Yes"

Matthew doesn't say another word he simply slides his arm around my waste before lifting me and carrying me down the hall where Connor had headed.

Placing my feet back on the floor as we crossed the threshold of our master suite, Matthew nods to Connor and lies on the bed. It was if they had their own secret language that I was yet to decipher.

"Now sweetheart, we have been easy on you so far. We aren't pushed you past what we thought you couldn't handle but we are Dom's after all and it's time to push your limits." Connor voice seemed to drop even over and sexier then I had ever heard from in all the years of knowing him.

I chance a look at Matthew and he's watching me with intent.

"Baby you said you wanted us both, it's your choice. If you want this you need to tell us."

"Yes" no thought required in my reply, this was what I wanted. My men.

"Climbing on baby"

I scramble to climb on Matthew lowering myself onto his already hard cock.

"Ahh"

"You love this, Sarah," Matthew grits out, smiling up at me with fierce heat.

"You were made for this. For us."

"Yes," I manage, rocking on top of him. Back against Matthew. Over and over.

"Hold her still," Connor says to Matthew, his voice at my shoulder ragged. Raw. Matthew's hands tighten on my hips, halting my movement, but even holding still, I can feel the pulsing heat of his cock inside me, throbbing. Micro-thrusts of his hips.

Connor parts my cheeks and cool liquid surprises me before the warmth of Connors fingers circle my puckered rose. Matthew slow starts to me again.

"Oh fuck" I moan as he push a finger past the tight ring. Fasten his pace below me Matthew kisses me as two more fingers enter me. My core tightens instantly. The digging pressure of

Matthew's fingers into my curves. It's intoxicating.

Connor's fingers pull out, and I whimper at the loss, turning to look at him over my shoulder. The look on his face... oh God. It almost tips me over the edge into another climax, and Matthew hisses below me, feeling the flutter of my inner muscles.

Fire floods through my belly, washes away the last of my nerves at what we're about to do. And then the fat head of his cock presses gently against my rear entrance. It feels amazing. Terrifying. I'm hungry for it. I swallow hard. Oh, God—this is really happening!

"Relax, sweetheart." Connor says gently, his hands running up my thighs, fingertips grazing over the place where we connect so sweetly.

"Relax, we've got you."

The look in his eyes captures me, steadies me, drives the lust inside me even higher. I see desire and care and the same golden feeling of perfection, of belonging, that I feel every time the three of us are together. I let out a shaky breath and relax back into his hands, trusting him.

Chapter 18

Connor

It had been with months since the night that I first shared Sarah with Matthew and as I looked down at Sarah soundlessly sleeping between Matthew and I, I finally felt like life was complete. Sure it had been one hell of a roller coaster ride but it had all been worth it. Matthew and I had to just become better friends but we were closer now than ever. Sarah was ours. It all fell into place. I rented out my place in the suburbs and moved into the penthouse. Katherine was delighted that she had two daddy's, saying " it as the coolest ever because meant she go more ice cream and princess days". Of course she did. Our little girl.

We all agreed that since Sarah couldn't legally be married to both Matthew and I that, Sarah would take my collar and that both Katherine and her would hyphenate their names to share with my own. But it was the collaring ceremony that made our family complete.

Highclere was buzzing. I'd rarely seen so many members crammed into it, not even for the traditional Australia Day party. The area around the stage was packed. Jackson, Declan and Rhys the club owners were waiting for us there. The whisper of chatter died away as Matthew and I led Sarah through the crowd to where Rhys stood.

Once on the stage, we stood next to Rhys and waited for him to speak.

"It's wonderful to see so many of you here to witness and share in Connor and Sarah's union. I cannot tell you what a joy it has been to watch the man I trained finally find the one who completes him." He nodded toward Declan. Declan smiled.

"It has been a privilege to see Sarah blossom into the person he was truly meant to be. Theirs has not been an easy journey, but the fact that we are all here tonight to witness Sarah's collaring is a cause for celebration." Rhys and Declan stepped back, allowing Sarah and me to take centre stage. I gazed at Sarah who was quivering

with excitement.

"Strip, Sarah." she removed dress, until at last he was naked, standing upright, completely at ease. I went to take off her training collar I had given her months ago, but Sarah reached up to stop me.

"What's the matter, sweetheart?" I whispered to him.

"I... I can't. Please, I don't want to lose this. It connects me to you." her eyes were pleading with me. I wanted to scoop her up and hold her close.

"It's okay, Sarah. We're going to keep that collar at home. It's never going away, and it will always be important to you. But I hope what I have for you will become even more important. Will you trust me?" She met my gaze, and I was floored by the look of naked trust in those expressive blue eyes.

"I trust you, Sir." He stood quietly as I unfastened the collar and handed it to Matthew. I looked to the left of the stage, where Rhys and Declan were waiting. I gave Rhys a nod, and he stepped up onto the stage, trembling slightly. When he reached me, he held out the box I had given him earlier and then stepped away, quickly retreating to where Declan stood. I turned to Sarah.

"Kneel." Sarah dropped slowly to her knees, her

posture perfect.

"You've been my sub for months, and I'm proud to make you mine for always."

Sarah's face glowed. I removed the curved polished chrome collar from its box and held it up for Sarah to see. Her eyes lit up. I gave her a nod. Sarah cleared her throat.

"I kneel before you, Sir, and offer myself to you. I am bound to you by more than earthly bonds. I don't have much to offer you but these three things." her eyes shone.

"I give you my body. It's yours, to do with as you see fit. " Sarah paused. I stared at her in rapt attention. She hadn't revealed her vows to me, wanting them to remain a surprise.

"I give you my heart, knowing it will be in safe hands. And I give you my mind, with all that I feel for you." she smiled, and it tugged at my heart. "I give you all these things, in the certain knowledge that they will be safe in your keeping." She lifted her chin and locked eyes with me.

"My only desire is to serve you, to please you. Where you lead, I will follow, for the rest of our life together."

I swallowed, fighting to hold back the tears that threatened to overwhelm me. Sarah looked meaningfully at me. I'd been so overcome with emotion, I'd almost missed my cue. She grinned at me. My turn.

"Thank you for coming into my life and wanting to be mine. From this day on, you belong to me. You're a part of me, heart, body, and soul. I will cherish and protect you always. Your happiness and well-being are of vital importance to me, and I will do all I can to maintain these." I held out the collar.

"You kneel at my feet in submission. Accept this symbol of my love, devotion and ownership to wear as a sign of our commitment to each other, for all to see."

I bent and slipped the collar around her neck, and fastened it at the back. Sarah reached up to touch it, running her fingers over the smooth, cool metal, as if assuring himself it was really there. I help but smile.

"You're ours, Sarah." And then I cupped her cheek and kissed her. The applause broke out as Sarah surrendered to the kiss, her eyes closing as she lost himself in it.

Our lips parted, and I held out a hand to help Sarah to her feet. When the applause increased, I held up a hand for silence. Sarah gazed at me quizzically. Both Matthew and I turned to face her, grabbing both her hands.

"Sarah, everyone here knows by this collar that you

*are mine. But the outside world doesn't. And I want
everyone to know how much you mean to both Matthew
and I not just as my submissive, but also as our wife."*

*I gave Matthew a tiny nod, and he stepped up onto
the stage. Sarah's eyes widened as he caught sight of the
ring box which Declan handed to me—but that was
nothing compared to her reaction when both Matthew
and I got down on one knee and held out the box. Her
jaw dropped, but the ecstatic look in her eyes…. I
swallowed.*

*"Sarah Davidson, wear this ring that shows our love
is intertwined. That Matthew, and I love you beyond the
constraints of marriage and that you are more precious
to us than our next breath" I held my breath as Matthew
and I hadn't told Sarah anything about what we had
planned.*

*Looking from Matthew to myself, I could see the love
and emotion pouring from Sarah.*

*"Yes" leaning down to take a hand from each of us
"with great love, trust and honour will a wear this
ring."*

Sarah movement between brought my attention
to Matthew. His hand on her heavily pregnant

belly soothing her. Only a month before our son would be born and although I know not biologically mine they would never go without the love I have for him.

The End

About J.F. Lowe

I grew up in a country town in Outback, Australia. As the fruit of a long line of military men and not much to do, it gave me plenty of time to create a fantasy world full of hot men and wild romances. It was only when I met my own hot alpha that I decided to share my love of books and writing with the world.

Nowadays, I in Brisbane, Australia and when I'm not writing, I can be found with a nice glass of wine and spends her time with her husband and holidaying with her three children. My favourite way to spend an evening is curled up on a couch next to my own hot alpha, reading and making the most of a quiet night in… well maybe not so quiet... if

you read my books then you know what I
mean.

Get social with me!

Website: http://www.jflowe.com

VIP Reader Newsletter: http://www.jflowe.com/newsletter/

Facebook Author Page:https://www.facebook.com/J.F.LoweAuthor

Instagram: https://www.instagram.com/j.f.loweauthor/

Twitter:https://twitter.com/jflowe_author

Amazon Author:https://www.amazon.com/J.F.-Lowe/e/B07Q7B1NXD/

BookBub:https://www.bookbub.com/profile/j-f-lowe

Goodreads:https://www.goodreads.com/author/show/19028143.J_F_Lowe

Book+Main:https://bookandmainbites.com/JFLowe

Keep in touch by engaging with me through

one of the links above.

Subscribe to my VIP Readers newsletter for exclusive excerpts

Series by J.F. Lowe

Love Games Trilogy:
Married Games
Revenge Games
Sinful Games

Protecting Her Innocence (Standalone)

Seducing Series (Coming 2020):

Seducing Austin
Seducing Vegas
Seducing Philly

Road to Love Series (Coming 2020):

Broken Love
Departed Love
Forbidden Love

Series writing as Nancy Drew - Author

Masters of Highclere:

A Sailors Daughter
Coxswains Cuffs
Returning to Highclere
Medical Ménage

Review

If you enjoyed this book, please review it or recommend it to others so they can find it, too.

www.ingramcontent.com/pod-product-compliance
Lightning Source LLC
Chambersburg PA
CBHW061938130726
47909CB00013B/2034